A Bluegrass GIRL

and Other Horse Stories for Girls

A Bluegrass GIRL

and Other Horse Stories for Girls

Compiled and Edited by

JOE WHEELER

Published by eChristian, Inc.
Escondido, California

Mission 🏛 Books

A Bluegrass Girl and Other Horse Stories for Girls

First printing in 2012 by eChristian, Inc.
eChristian, Inc.
2235 Enterprise Street, Suite 140
Escondido, CA 92029
http://echristian.com

ISBN: 978-1-61843-218-6

Visit Joe Wheeler's website at www.joewheelerbooks.com.

Published in association with the WordServe Literary Group, Inc., 10152 Knoll Circle, Highlands Ranch, CO 80310, www.wordserveliterary.com.

Cover design by Mary Bellus.
Interior design by Larry Taylor.

Produced with the assistance of The Livingstone Corporation. Project staff includes: Dan Balow, Afton Rorvik, Dave Veerman, Linda Taylor, Linda Washington, Ashley Taylor, Andy Culbertson, Joel Bartlett, Lois Jackson, Sheila Urban, and Tom Shumaker.

Printed in the United States of America

19 18 17 16 15 14 13 12 8 7 6 5 4 3 2 1

Mission 🏠 Books

CONTENTS

INTRODUCTION

Girls and Horses
Joseph Leininger Wheeler

Girls and horses have an almost mystical bond. But it is different today from what it was in days gone by when horses were part of daily life, when they were necessities rather than luxuries. In fact, on the frontier, a horse often represented the difference between life and death; that is why, in the Old West, stealing one's horse was a hanging offense!

Today's world is very different. So much so that few girls are lucky enough to actually own a horse. Let me rephrase that: no one ever "owns" a horse, for it has to be give and take on both sides. But not to worry: for all those untold thousands of girls who can only wish they had a horse of their own, there are stories, story collections such as this one, and books about horses that can fill the gap.

Interestingly enough, girls have a definite time period during which horses come into their lives. It tends to begin when they are around eight or nine and lasts in full intensity until they are around fourteen—when boys begin demanding equal time.

But even then, the love between girl and horse rarely ceases with puberty, for the girl-woman never forgets this first love, and it thus enriches all the later years of her life. It is reinforced by passing on this love to her children and grandchildren, surprisingly often, bequeathing them her own *Velveteen Rabbit*-cherished and read-to-death horse books.

Walter Farley's horse novels come to life again for each generation of girls, as do the books of other writers of horse stories, both real and fictional. Rarely do girls begin with full-length novels, however, but rather they start with chapter books, then graduate to longer stories. Horse poetry too—I'll come back to that later in this book.

How This Book Came to Be

You may have noticed that books of unputdownable horse stories for girls are mighty hard to find. And I've been asked so often to search out a number of them and gather them into one collection, that this book became a reality.

I've been putting together story collections for a long time; in fact, this will be my sixty-fifth—well, make that "our" sixty-fifth, as my wife Connie loves horses too, and she's my partner in putting story collections together. So, if you like the stories in this collection, chances are you may want to check out my other story collections.

You can't get any luckier than I have been: I was born to a mother who loved stories and poetry and readings. In fact, believe it or not, she'd memorized by heart thousands of pages of stories and poems, knowing in their entirety book-length poems such as Longfellow's *Hiawatha* and *Evangeline!* Mother was what they used to call an "elocutionist," a stage performer who'd stand up in front of audiences and bring to life her favorite stories and poems. But she also did this for me, my brother Romayne, and my sister Marjorie. By "bring to life," I mean that she so immersed herself in whoever was in her stories that we'd enter her world and lose all track of reality during those performances—they were *that* real. And she passed on this love of story to each of us.

The thing I love best about stories is that I get to meet so many fascinating people, animals, and places, both real ones and once-upon-a-time ones. Climb into a time machine and travel back to a different world peopled by men, women, children, and animals that were just as real as we are today. That's just what we can do with the stories in this collection. We travel back in time as far back as our Revolutionary War almost 250 years ago; we relive the bloodiest war America ever fought, the Civil War; we experience the tumultuous times of the Old West when horses ruled supreme; we're there when automobiles came in and rudely started displacing horses; and we also experience a more familiar world, a world where we love and interact with horses for their own sakes, not just because we need them in order to survive. All of these worlds you will find in this collection.

Welcome aboard.

Coda

I'd love to hear from you after you've read these stories. Tell me which stories you liked most, and why. And tell me about your life and what you enjoy most. You might even suggest other types of story collections you'd like to see me put together. Just address your letter to

> Dr. Joe
> P.O. Box 1246
> Conifer, Colorado 80433

Or find us on our website: www.joewheelerbooks.com.

◆◆◆

A Bluegrass GIRL

William H. Woods

Red Lass—why was Tamsy's brother Tom riding the horse in the middle of the night? When she later discovered the reason—everything changed.

Tamsy was just turning away from the window when she caught a glimpse of a figure on the lawn. The moon was nearly down, and the shadows of the maples were so deep, that she could not be certain she had seen anything. But, looking intently, she saw, now beyond a doubt, a mounted horseman move across the grass. It was the time of the Night Riders in Kentucky, and for a moment the girl was startled. But she soon recognized her brother, Tom, on his young saddle horse, Red Lass; and for some minutes, Tamsy, at her dark window, watched the Lass racking, single-footing, cantering, and moving at any other gait the most accomplished Kentucky saddle animal is supposed to have. Tamsy did not know what it meant. But she knew that Tom was devoted to the young horse he had raised, and lately broken for his own use and that it was not at all beyond him to go out at midnight for a little practice. The girl turned away at length with a smile, and an unspoken wish that her only brother was not quite so fond of horses.

Tamsy was to start the next morning for Louisville, to begin her last year at school, and the comedy on the dark lawn slipped her memory for a little while. Tamsy's school life had been very successful. She had taken and kept her place at the head of the class with a quiet confidence rather unusual in one so young; and she had, moreover, developed literary ability that had attracted attention outside her school circle. She was going back now with bright anticipation, enhanced by the fact that for a while it had looked as if she were not to go back at all. The Coyles were far from being wealthy, and it had only been within the fortnight, and after vigorous effort, that Tom had been able to manage it.

"I can't imagine yet how he raised the money," she said at the breakfast table next morning, "and I feel as if I couldn't thank him enough. I wish he hadn't hurried off before I started. What took him to town so early, Mother?"

"It's court day in Lexington," Mrs. Coyle answered, "and Tom had business there he was anxious about; and he thought he had better bid you good-by last night."

"I saw a good deal of him after the good-by," said Tamsy, smiling; and she told her mother of the midnight ride.

Mrs. Coyle listened with evident interest; but, to Tamsy's surprise, seemed rather troubled than amused.

"You don't appreciate the funny side of it as I do, Mother," she said at last. "But I wouldn't mind. Tom's a dear, good boy, but you know he always was a tiny bit horsy."

A rare pink came into Mrs. Coyle's cheeks, and she looked up with shining eyes.

"Tom may not have quite the same tastes you have, Tamsy," said she, "and he has not gone to college because his health would not allow it and because there was not money enough for you both. But if you think I am troubled by what you call your brother's horsy ways, you are very much mistaken. He is only a year older than you, and, ignorant as we are of business affairs, I do not know what would have become of us if it had not been for Tom."

Tamsy made quick amends for her speech, and parted from her mother with all the old affection. But the conversation awakened questions in the girl's mind that would not go away. Had she abused their affection and their pride in her success? Had she been selfish? She could not find in her own mind a wholly satisfactory answer.

Madam Donan, principal of Edgewood Seminary, in the suburbs of Louisville, and Miss Jackson, professor of belles lettres, were in the parlor when Tamsy reached Edgewood.

"A hearty welcome, Mr. President," said Madam, kissing the girl's cheek. "Should I say 'Mr. President' or 'Miss President,' Miss Jackson? I hardly know which is correct."

"Neither, just yet, I should say," was Miss Jackson's reply. "Have you had a pleasant summer, Miss Coyle?"

"Delightful," said Tamsy, and added some polite inquiry about Miss Jackson's vacation. But the flush that had risen in her cheeks at Miss Jackson's remark was slow to leave. That remark, and Madam's as well, voiced, it was true, the general impression that Tamsy would be the new class president; but it annoyed the girl to have it thus publicly taken for granted.

It soon became clear, however, that Tamsy would be elected without opposition. But as the presidency meant inevitable additional expense, and the getting back to school at all had been so doubtful, her election was a possibility she had not mentioned at home. Happily for Tamsy, just at this time, a story she had entered in a magazine competition won a prize of one hundred dollars. She was glad to be able to write home, therefore, that the presidency would mean no more expense to them.

The class election was still a fortnight away when Tamsy went into Louisville with Miss Jackson on a shopping trip. As they were turning into Fourth Street, they heard a sudden noise, cries, and shouts, with the quick trampling of hoofs; and the next instant, a plunging, rearing horse, hitched to a doctor's phaeton, dashed into sight. The driver was using the whip, and the horse, mad with pain and fright, reared straight up in the air, and, losing its balance, fell to the pavement with a crash.

Miss Jackson, who was on the crossing, instantly darted back to the sidewalk, dragging Tamsy by the arm. But, to her amazement, the girl pulled herself free, stepped quickly into the street, and took hold of the bridle reins close by the bit, and still held them when the trembling animal struggled to its feet—Tamsy had recognized Red Lass!

"Whoa, Lass! Steady, girl, steady!" she said, stroking with one hand the horse's neck, while with the other she clung to the bridle. "Put down that whip!" she called to the astonished driver, and turned again to her task of soothing the horse.

The thing had happened so quickly that Miss Jackson had been speechless. But now she cried out, "Miss Coyle, I insist that you come away from there at once. This is ridiculous!"

Tamsy did not seem to hear. The groom had now scrambled out of the phaeton, and went to the horse's head.

"Look at those great welts there on her side," Tamsy said to him, with flashing eyes. "How could you? How dare you?"

"Dr. Cantrell told me to hook her up," said the astonished groom, "and she got scared—"

"Dr. Cantrell?" said Tamsy. "What Dr. Cantrell?"

"Dr. Cantrell round here on Walnut Street."

Dr. Cantrell the master of Red Lass! It suddenly flashed across her mind that this was how Tom had raised the money to send her back to school.

"Here, then," said Tamsy, opening her purse, "here's carfare for you to ride home. I'll drive the horse back myself. I'm sorry if I spoke to you too sharply, but this horse was my brother's pet, and is not used to being beaten."

"Miss Coyle, I positively forbid your trying to drive that beast," said Miss Jackson. "I insist on your getting out of that carriage at once. This may be a serious business for you."

Tamsy was already in the phaeton. "It is serious now, Miss Jackson, more so than you think," she replied. "Give her her head, please," she called to the groom, and started up the street. She had a dim impression of someone's coming up quickly and of a man's voice calling after her; but Red Lass required all her attention, and she did not look back.

Dr. Cantrell was out when she reached the office, and turning the horse over to the office boy, Tamsy made her way back to Edgewood.

The story of her adventure had preceded her. "I have always thought Miss Coyle a typical southerner, with her soft manners and slow speech," Miss Jackson, herself a Michigan woman, was saying to Madam, "but I shall never again doubt that such manners may go with efficiency. That man dropped that whip as if it burned him; and she got into the buggy and drove off in spite of me, and everybody else; and she had tears in her eyes all the while."

Tamsy was near to tears again when she made her explanation to Madam and Miss Jackson. But, unusual as her conduct had been, she would probably have heard no more of it if that had been all; but it was not. She wanted to go and see Dr. Cantrell; and of that Madam strongly disapproved.

"I think the matter must end here," she said, "and, at any rate, I can give it no further attention now. Mrs. Weems has just had a bad fall, and I am waiting to learn how serious it is."

It proved that Mrs. Weems, the housekeeper, had broken a leg, a misfortune not only for her, but for the large household under her care.

After recitation hours the next day, Tamsy went to Miss Jackson. "Are you very busy?" Tamsy asked.

"Not unusually so," was the reply. "What is it?"

"Would you be willing to go to Dr. Cantrell with me? I feel that I must see him."

Miss Jackson frankly stared. "What?" she said coldly. "When I am a teacher in the school, and myself heard the principal forbid your going?"

"But I am going to leave the school immediately," said Tamsy, "and I shall tell Madam today that I am going."

"Going to leave school!" Miss Jackson exclaimed. "Is it possible that after your three years of success here and your bright prospects, you will throw everything away for a horse? You Kentuckians are impossible!"

"Not altogether for a horse," Tamsy answered. "But I reckon it does take a Kentuckian to understand Kentuckians," she added, with a wan little smile.

Finally, however, Miss Jackson consenting, they presented themselves in Dr. Cantrell's office.

Tamsy introduced her companion and herself. "We saw the runaway yesterday," she said, "and have come to speak to you about the horse."

"And are you the young lady who took her away from the groom and drove her home?" asked the tall, clerical-looking old gentleman.

"I—I didn't mean to take her away from anyone," said Tamsy, blushing. "But, you see, I helped raise the horse, and I thought she knew me—and I—I could—"

"You could, and you did," said Dr. Cantrell, his blue eyes twinkling upon her. "I suppose there is no possible way of inducing you to take charge of the horse altogether?"

"That's what I came to see about," was the unexpected reply. "Dr. Cantrell, will you sell me Red Lass?"

"Not I," he answered with a promptness his smiling face belied. "Not a crusty, close-fisted old chap like me, who knows when he has got a bargain. My son, Hugh, now, might not be so hard to deal with."

"Does he own Red Lass?"

"Partly; or thinks he does. Ah, here he comes to speak for himself," he added, as a tall young man entered the office. "Hugh, here is your unknown of yesterday; and she wants to buy your horse."

Tamsy's cheeks were crimson, and her speech, at first, unsteady, but her eyes did not falter once. She had not understood, she said, that it was Mr. Cantrell who called after her the day before; she disapproved of the groom and his whip, and that was why she did what she did. As for her errand today, she explained with a proud simplicity, and as briefly as possible, that Red Lass had been the pet and chief possession of her brother, always delicate and dependent upon an active outdoor life; and that the Lass had been sacrificed for Tamsy's benefit, as she had just now discovered.

"I have only a hundred dollars with me," she ended with a shy eagerness, "but if you will keep the horse, and wait until I can raise the balance—Mr. Cantrell? I—I—mean, of course," she hesitated, "how much do you ask for Red Lass?"

"I gave your brother four hundred dollars for her," said Hugh, and he turned to his father. "Miss Coyle gets the horse, of course?" he said.

There was no need of any payment now, they said; but Tamsy insisted on turning over her beloved prize check. "And the balance I'll pay just as soon as I can," she said.

On the way home, Miss Jackson tried her utmost to lend Tamsy money, but it was steadily refused. "If you had told Madam the half of what you told those two strangers, you would not have had to leave school," she remonstrated.

"But isn't that old gentleman a dear?" Tamsy cried. "And you are another!" she added, patting her companion's arm. "But I should have left school in any case, Miss Jackson. I have that three hundred dollars to raise."

She said nothing of any plan she had in mind; but that evening Madam was told that someone wished to see her about the housekeeper's place. "I do not understand," said Madam. "I only sent in the advertisement this afternoon."

Her face flushed with surprise and displeasure when Tamsy rose to meet her in the parlor. But she heard the girl's stammering plea to the end. After all, the idea was not wholly presumptuous. Tamsy only wanted to come on trial, and as assistant housekeeper.

"Since you have chosen to come to me in this way, Miss Coyle," said Madam, at last, "I shall meet you on your own ground. My housekeeper buys all the food and fuel supplies for the establishment and has a position of great responsibility. You have had experience in this line of work?" Madam continued, with eyes that twinkled kindly as she regarded Tamsy's downcast face.

Madam Donan, for all her wisdom and experience, was still, at times, an impulsive woman. She got up quickly, and taking Tamsy by both hands, exclaimed: "Now you dear little goose, sit down here, and tell me what has got into you, in these last two days! Housekeeper, indeed!"

Nevertheless, Tamsy gained her point, but only after a long talk and certain very strict provisos. Mrs. Coyle was to approve, first of all, although, of course, no syllable was to be breathed to Tom. Then the agreement was to last only until Christmas but with full salary if Tamsy succeeded. Best of all, by leaving off some extra studies, and all outside work, Tamsy might still be able to retain her place in the class, although the presidency must go by the board. "And if you will get into the good graces of Mrs. Weems, and let her advise with you, I am sure you will make a success of it," Madam concluded.

The prophecy was fulfilled. There were mistakes, to be sure, some costly ones. But Tamsy brought to her new work the same intelligence and sometimes even more of eagerness, than she was used to bring to her studies; and it was soon evident that she could not fail.

She begged off for a day or two at Christmas; and, all unannounced, got off the Lexington train at her home station late one afternoon.

"Did my horse come, Mr. Harms?" she called out eagerly to the agent.

Yes; Red Lass was waiting there in the stable. Mr. Harms had his trap all ready, too, and would drive Miss Tamsy home right away. And the horse he would send over at twilight, and have her hitched at the rack, just as Miss Tamsy had written. But he did not quite carry out this plan, for Tom's amazed eyes saw Red Lass before she got to the hitching rack; and then, of course, came Tamsy's explanation.

"And to think," she ended, whispering the words to her brother, "I laughed at you; laughed at you! And thought you 'horsy.' But I didn't know—I didn't know!"

Tom was in great straits. His gulping refusal to take the horse had been utterly ignored.

"But look here, you people," he cried, "do you think I prefer any horse that ever walked to my sister?"

"And I? Am I to prefer college honors to my brother?" was the reply.

Tom stared a moment helplessly, and then suddenly seized her in a brotherly bear hug, and rushed out of the house.

But late, late that night, Tamsy imagined she heard a sound outside, and, with a sudden thought, got up and went to the window. And down at the bottom of the lawn, between the shadows of the naked maple trees, a horseman went riding to and fro across the grass.

And Tom's happiness was not to be Tamsy's only reward, for the next summer when she was at home again, having brought back with her all the honors that Edgewood Seminary could confer upon her, Tom insisted on sharing his pet with her, and so she too had many a glorious canter mounted on Red Lass.

◢◢◢

Oatsey REMEMBERS

L. R. Davis

Oh to ride a grand horse like White Sox! Instead she was stuck on that polo-scarred Oatsey. When Sally was offered the opportunity of riding White Sox instead, she jumped at the chance.

Then she looked into her brother's face . . .

The crisp call of the bugle announced the beginning of the local saddle horse class. Patsy Cameron waved to Freddy, gave her pony an encouraging little pat, and followed the other riders into the show ring.

"Walk, please," the announcer called to the prancing line that circled around the bunting-draped judge's stand. That was easy, Patsy thought, sitting up very straight in the saddle. Now that Oatsey was an old gentleman he liked to walk.

"Trot, please," came the next command. Oatsey didn't like that so well. He was a retired polo pony, and he thought anything less than a fast canter was a waste of time. One after another of the horses churned bits of dirt up into Oatsey's gray face as they trotted proudly past. Patsy hurried him along as fast as she could and tried not to look to where her brother Freddy's wheelchair was pulled up to the edge of the ring. In spite of all their training, Oatsey's gaits just weren't right for a show horse.

"Walk, please!" Oatsey stopped with a jolt. "Canter" was coming next, Patsy knew. All summer long Freddy had been coaching her on how to make Oatsey behave at just this moment. Freddy's knees had had to be operated on in the spring, so he couldn't ride himself. It was up to Patsy to make Oatsey do his best.

"Canter," the announcer boomed. Patsy urged Oatsey forward with her left toe while she held him gently back on the right curb. There! His inside white foot was leading off with the regularity of a rocking horse. Patsy held her breath. If she could only keep him down to a slow collected canter everything would be all right.

The third time round the ring Patsy gave a sigh of relief. Even Freddy would be satisfied. If Oatsey was going too fast for a show horse, he was doing wonderfully well for an ex–polo pony.

After a few minutes of cantering they were ordered into a line in the center of the ring. Patsy found herself between the Athertons' show mare White Sox and a gleaming bay belonging to the Parsons. Patsy patted Oatsey hard on the little bald spot in front of the saddle. Standing next to White Sox he looked more than ever like a small gray mouse. Patsy made him bring his feet together, but nothing could force him to stretch in a fashionable arch with his front feet and his hind feet spread wide apart. Oatsey left that sort of nonsense to show horses.

The judge came past and glanced down his long nose at Oatsey's scarred legs. Patsy felt uncomfortable. Oatsey'd gotten every one of those marks playing polo, and Freddy proudly called them his medals. Patsy knew that they weren't exactly beautiful, but the judge didn't have to look as though they smelled.

Soon it was all over, and the blue ribbon fluttered from White Sox's bridle. Patsy followed the other losers out of the ring. She put on Oatsey's halter and blanket and left him in his temporary stall while she went to see Freddy.

He was leaning back in his chair looking pleased. "You were all right," he said, "and Oatsey was swell. I'd just like to see him with those mincing thoroughbreds along a country road. He'd show 'em up."

Patsy wandered off to find out what time her next class began. She was glad that Freddy was so crazy about his pony that he was satisfied just to see him going decently. For herself Patsy felt just a little bit of disappointment making a hard ring in her throat.

"Oh, Miss Patsy!" It was Jake Prince, the Athertons' groom, running toward her on putteed legs that looked so thin Patsy wondered if they wouldn't break. "Mr. Atherton wants to see you."

"What for?" Patsy asked.

Jake kept right on running to where Mr. Atherton was standing with another man watching the "Touch-and-Go" jumping class. "He's looking for a jockey," was all he would say.

"Patsy, this is Major Wicks." Mr. Atherton introduced the judge of the local saddle horse class. "Major, this is the young lady I want to have ride White Sox in the class for saddle mares, ladies to ride."

The major looked down at Patsy from over a very white, very stiff stock. "I'm sorry I'm not judging that," he said. "I'd like to see you properly mounted."

Patsy was so excited about riding White Sox that she didn't even feel insulted for Oatsey. There wasn't a girl in Monmouth County who wouldn't have given anything to ride that big, dazzling chestnut. "D'you really mean me?" Patsy asked, and Mr. Atherton said he did. That settled it. Freddy would approve because Oatsey wasn't eligible for that class anyway.

In almost no time Jake was giving her a leg up onto White Sox's shining back. "All set, Patsy?" Mr. Atherton asked as he shortened one stirrup and Jake shortened the other. Patsy nodded and Major Wicks patted White Sox with a professional hand. "Just ride her as though she were that moth-eaten little roan you rode before," the major said.

Patsy was glad Freddy hadn't heard that. Just then the bugle blew again, and White Sox gave a little impatient prance to be off. "All right," Patsy said, gripping very tight with her knees, and instantly Mr. Atherton and Jake stood back. It felt a little like riding on a piece of dynamite, but Patsy was enough of a horsewoman to enjoy every bit of it. Mr. Atherton took off his hat and the major saluted, and White Sox bounded into the ring with Patsy feeling more like a young lady than she'd ever felt before in her life.

It was all new and strange and thrilling. In the first place there was the delicious excitement of riding an unfamiliar horse. In the second place, from the minute White Sox stepped saucily into the ring, the judge was watching her and admiring her and checking up her merits.

She went through the walk, trot, walk, and canter almost perfectly. Once a program fluttered across the ring, and White Sox shied awkwardly away from it. Patsy quickly had her in hand, but she couldn't help wondering what it would be like to ride her on the road where anything was likely to happen.

They lined up and White Sox arched like a bow without even being urged. Patsy patted her approvingly, but somehow she felt that it didn't make much difference. White Sox was perfectly sure of her own superiority anyway.

"Number sixty-seven to the front, please." Almost without Patsy's moving, White Sox wheeled out of line and trotted in front of the other horses to the judge's stand. The announcer fastened a deep blue rosette to her bridle and handed Patsy a silver cup. Patsy said "Thank you" and trotted sedately around the ring as though it happened every day. Inside she was perfectly ready to burst. She caught Freddy's eye and he looked pleased. But then, he had looked just as pleased when Oatsey had cantered on the right foot.

Mr. Atherton and Jake were properly excited. Even Major Wicks seemed less stiff than his own tall field boots. He shook her hand and then told her she'd put up a jolly good performance.

Mr. Atherton waited until the major left them to go back to the judge's stand and then turned to Patsy. "You'll ride White Sox in the class for horsemanship, won't you?" he said. "The major's judging that, and you'll have a better chance on a showy-looking mount even though the horse isn't supposed to count."

Patsy nodded, watching Jake leading White Sox away with the blue ribbon still fluttering proudly from her bridle. "I'd just love it," she said. "Oatsey's sweet but he isn't exactly a show pony."

"No," said Mr. Atherton dryly. "Not exactly."

When Patsy reached Freddy's chair he was sitting up very straight watching a harness class. "You were great," he said. "Let's see the cup."

"The Athertons kept it," Patsy said. "People usually do when it's the horse."

"Of course," said Freddy. Neither of them admitted how much a cup would have added to the Camerons' stable, which as yet had no trophies in it at all.

"There's still the horsemanship class," Patsy said.

Freddy's round brown eyes lighted up his thin face. "You bet," he said. "And with the way you manage Oatsey now, I shouldn't wonder a bit if you had a good chance."

"But the horse doesn't count," Patsy said slowly.

"No, it doesn't, not for itself; but if you do a good job riding it, why that's a lot."

Patsy could almost see White Sox flashing around that ring. The minute she came in sight you couldn't help noticing her and whoever was on her back. When Oatsey was in the ring, nobody seemed to know that he existed. "What would you think of not putting Oatsey in the horsemanship class?" she asked.

Freddy looked away from the harness class he had been watching. "Why, what do you mean?" he said. "After all the practicing we did this summer and all?"

Patsy thought of Freddy's being wheeled down to the south pasture and spending afternoon after afternoon in the hot sun to coach Oatsey and herself. "Of course, you're the one that's going to do the riding," Freddy was saying. "You can do whatever you want."

"And I want to ride Oatsey!" Patsy said, and shut her mouth tight. In a minute she hurried off to the stables without saying another word.

She went straight to where a long line of blue and red and yellow ribbons marked White Sox's stall, but Mr. Atherton was not there. She hurried past without even looking inside for fear she might be tempted to change her mind. Freddy and Oatsey between them had taught her everything she knew about riding. If Freddy counted on seeing her riding his horse, then that was that. It was only not riding White Sox that made it hard.

She found Mr. Atherton just coming into the stable and told him as quickly as she could that she had changed her mind.

"But old Wicks is mad about White Sox," Mr. Atherton said when she'd finished. "His eye'll be on her the minute you come into the ring. In a class of over forty youngsters, that's worth thinking about."

Patsy knew it was well worth thinking about. But she shook her head. "You see, my brother," she began, but then realized that there wasn't much point in telling Mr. Atherton just what Freddy thought about Oatsey. Mr. Atherton just didn't feel that way about horses. "And I'd really better not," she finished lamely.

Mr. Atherton looked offended.

"If the mare's given you a rough ride before I could understand it, but as it is I must say I don't. Still, I expect I shan't have much trouble finding someone else who'll jump at riding her."

Patsy watched him walk off, and her jodhpur boot traced little uncertain patterns in the dirt stable floor. There wasn't the slightest doubt about anybody else's jumping at the chance.

It wasn't until the horsemanship class had actually begun that Patsy found out it was Sally Parsons who Mr. Atherton had gotten to ride White Sox. Patsy watched them bounding into the ring and saw that Major Wicks was already following them through his thick eyeglass. Sally was two years younger than Patsy, and she had already won several ribbons that day with her own horse. In spite of every resolution to be a good sport, it wasn't any fun to have Sally riding by with White Sox's haughty heels kicking turf in Oatsey's face.

They did the usual things, and Oatsey did his best although his trot was much too slow and his canter much too fast. Then the announcer called everybody into the middle of the ring and had a whispered conversation with Major Wicks.

When he took up his megaphone again he had a lot to say. There were so many children in the class and so many good riders that it was very hard to judge. In order to be perfectly fair Major Wicks wanted to see all of them riding on regular road conditions. They were to follow the outside course by twos although of course not going over the jumps. Then they were to take a short stretch of rough road at the end of the showground and turn around and come back. They were to go at a fast trot and come back at a slow collected canter.

The announcer arranged the children in twos. Patsy found herself next to White Sox and bit her lip as the larger horse disdainfully arched her neck and pawed the ground. Oatsey looked smaller and humbler than ever.

They watched the first pair and the second. In the third pair one horse had a splendid swift trot and the other lagged awkwardly behind. Sally Parsons looked down at Oatsey and giggled. "That's the way we'll look except on the canter. Then it'll be the same thing only the other way round."

Patsy forced a grin. There wasn't much doubt that Oatsey's long loping canter would carry him home ahead no matter how she tried to make it look slow and collected and horse-showy.

"Step up, please," the announcer called. It was their turn next. Patsy didn't think about Freddy or Oatsey or anything except how much she wanted to have the earth open up and swallow her.

But the earth wouldn't oblige. In the very first few steps White Sox was ahead, her free showy trot carrying her hopelessly beyond Oatsey's awkward efforts. Once Patsy gave Oatsey a pronounced little kick, but he paid no attention and jogged on at his usual rate.

They got down to the short stretch of road at the end of the outside course. Patsy was just wishing they could begin cantering when she saw White Sox break into an unmistakable gallop.

A small white terrier had run out across the road. White Sox wasn't used to surprises and had dashed off before Sally could stop her. A show horse wasn't accustomed to meeting little white yapping dogs who had no respect for dainty thoroughbred legs.

Patsy expected to see Sally pull White Sox back into a trot. The dog went back off the road, but White Sox kept right on going. The dirt was coming up in clumps from her flying feet, and her head was down.

White Sox was running away!

Sally was trying to give and take on the reins, but it didn't do any good. Once the great chestnut mare had made up her mind to go, the light show bridle was useless in holding her.

Patsy hesitated for a moment. Oatsey was still going at his own safe pace. The dog barked at him, but Oatsey only cocked his ears forward and went on. Patsy knew that if they went on a little further and then came back cantering they would have as perfect a performance as Oatsey was capable of.

She looked ahead and saw that White Sox was still steaming over the ground. Once frightened, nothing could calm her. She was off the little dirt road now and running wildly across a field to the concrete state road that gleamed in the distance.

Patsy didn't wait another second. "Step on it, Oatsey," she urged. "We've got to stop her."

The small pony flattened out into a full loping gallop. Patsy could hardly feel the rise and fall of his small back as they raced along. This was what Oatsey had been taught as a young horse on the polo field, and it was still the thing he could do best.

White Sox made awkward work of the field, and they were gaining every minute. Still White Sox was plunging ahead, and Patsy could see a motor van roaring southward on the state road. The driver didn't see them, and there wasn't one chance in ten that Sally could swerve White Sox away from the road. She was sticking on to the saddle, and that took her every ounce of strength.

"Go, Oatsey!" Patsy urged. The little pony drew up to the mare just as she was reaching the road.

Patsy had one arm out for the reins, but Oatsey had ideas of his own. With his whole weight he shoved into White Sox!

For a minute Patsy's leg was crushed into White Sox's soft side. She could feel Sally's hair in her mouth and hear the grinding of the truck's brakes.

In another minute Oatsey had forced White Sox into a full turn. They were galloping back the way they had come.

Patsy gasped for breath as she straightened herself in the saddle. Oatsey had turned polo pony again and ridden White Sox off!

In the distance the truck was speeding on. At one side the white-washed jumps flashed past as Oatsey guided White Sox beside the outside course.

It wasn't anything like a hand collected gallop, but they were headed in the right direction. Oatsey thought it was a polo game, and there was no time to waste.

Almost before Patsy knew what had happened, they were back near the ring. Jake Prince ran out from the sidelines and swung onto White Sox's bridle. With nostrils wide and heels plunging the mare was forced to a standstill.

Oatsey stopped so suddenly Patsy slid up onto his neck. She tried to get him to go faster, but he walked the rest of the way home. As far as he was concerned the game was over.

Jake held onto White Sox while the rest of the horses were tried out and even led her into the line for the final prizegiving. It wasn't much of a showing of Sally's riding, and Patsy felt like getting off and asking Oatsey's pardon. Just then the announcer began calling her number and trying to put a ribbon onto Oatsey's small gray head. Oatsey thought ribbons were silly and objected strenuously. Finally Patsy had to carry the fluttering ribbon and the cup, too. "Well done," Major Wicks called as she trotted out of the ring. "Oh, very well done. Nice handy pony, too!"

Patsy rode straight over to Freddy's chair. He was so excited he was bouncing up and down with his stiff plaster-covered legs jouncing dangerously in front of him. "Oh, wonderful," he said. "Just swellegant! You've won the good horsemanship cup, and it's yours for keeps."

"Oatsey's," said Patsy firmly. "He won it all by himself. The ribbon goes over his stall, too, because he doesn't like 'em pinned to himself. Leaves that to lightweights like White Sox."

◆◆◆

Emily GEIGER

Nina N. Selivanova

The year was 1781, and the Revolutionary War was still waging. An urgent message needed to be sent to the American general, but it was almost certain death should the messenger be caught.

But Emily Geiger dared to carry it anyway.

Author's Note—In 1781, upon the soil of South Carolina, the last battles of the Revolution were fought, which resulted in the eviction of the British from the South. Many were the heroic deeds performed by individuals in those days, and Emily Geiger's ride should occupy a prominent place among them.

On an early summer morning in 1781, Emily Geiger came running into the room where her father lay bedridden.

"Father, Father," she cried, "I've just heard something, something very important."

"Go ahead," said John Geiger, smiling fondly at his only child, "tell me."

"I've heard," Emily lowered her voice, but it still vibrated with excitement, "that General Greene needs a messenger to carry a letter to General Sumter, and I'd like to offer my services."

"Spoken like a true patriot," remarked her father thoughtfully, "and I would be the last person to hinder you, but have you considered the danger of such an enterprise? The countryside is overrun by British and Tories. To avoid meeting them and being detained, you would have to go in a roundabout way, and don't you know that it's at least fifty miles to Sumter's camp, as the crow flies?"

"Of course, I know all that," retorted Emily with spirit, "but can't you see how much easier it would be for a girl to break through than for a man? Besides, can't I go a-visiting my best friend Abby and see her baby?" and Emily opened wide her large brown eyes and gave to her face an expression of such demure innocence that her father chuckled.

"I see," he said, "your mind is made up and you know all the answers."

"Oh, Father," exclaimed his daughter, "I knew you wouldn't object."

"How could I object?" There was a touch of bitterness in the sick man's voice. "If I am unable to serve my country, the least I can do is to let my daughter take my place."

"Oh, Father, please," protested Emily, patting his hand. "You shouldn't feel this way. You know you are doing your bit, and much more than that. . . . Everybody here looks up to you . . . follows your advice. . . ."

"Forget about me," interrupted Geiger. "Let's talk about you. When do you want to go?"

"Right away. And I may have to stay with Abby for a while, so don't worry about me. I'll send word to you as soon as I can."

"I know God is with us," replied Geiger, "and He will bless and keep you, my child."

Emily kissed him tenderly and ran out of the room.

About an hour or so later, Emily was already at Greene's camp, asking to see the general. Led into his presence she announced her intention of riding with the message.

Greene was delighted. No one knew better than he that to send a man to Sumter meant to send him to his death, for, once caught by the British or the Tories, he would certainly be hanged, whereas a girl . . . still that was hazardous too.

"Do you realize the danger you'll be facing while you are on the road?" he asked Emily.

"I do," she replied, "but then I know every path and byway here, for this is my home. I have a fleet horse which I have raised and broken myself, and I trust it will carry me all the way to General Sumter's camp. I am not afraid of the distance, for I am used to riding for miles and miles at a time. And," she added with a sly smile, "should I meet either British or Tories, I'll dare them to stop me—a simple country girl on her way to see her childhood friend, who has just had a baby!" Here Emily twisted her face and it assumed an expression of innocence bordering on stupidity.

General Greene burst out laughing. "That's the spirit!" he exclaimed. "If we had more men like this girl," he said to his officers, "there soon wouldn't be any British to fight with. I am now going to write the letter," he added and walked away.

In a few minutes he was back. "Here is the letter," he told Emily. "I will read it to you a few times, so that you can memorize it. Then, if you are caught, you can destroy the evidence and still be able to give the message to General Sumter. But there is time yet to change your mind, you know."

"I don't want to," Emily assured him. "I know I can get through."

She quickly memorized the letter and rode away. But, instead of making straight for Sumter's camp, she turned in the opposite direction. She knew that there were many volunteer spies among the Tory population on the Congaree River who watched Greene's camp with a hawk's eye. So, if any of these spies would see her, she told herself, they'd never guess where she was bound.

After a while, however, Emily halted at a crossroad and listened intently. The silence of the woods reassured her. Well, she was safe so far, for no one had followed her, she congratulated herself. Now she could steer her course straight for Sumter's camp. But she would have to keep to the old, sometimes half-obliterated, wood roads, even if it meant losing more precious time. She knew how well the main roads were patrolled.

For a time she proceeded without encountering anyone. Then, as she came to the end of a wood road, she hesitated for a moment. She could shorten her way by at least five miles if she were to take the highway. She looked around and strained her ears for some sound. The highway seemed deserted and silence reigned over it. Well, she'd take a chance, she decided, and rode forward. But a mile further she suddenly seemed to hear a faint sound of hoofbeats, beyond a curve in the road. She did not wait to investigate, but quickly plunged into the undergrowth. A moment later two British scouts came riding into view. They were apparently in a hurry and did not keep a sharp eye on the road. Emily heaved a sigh of relief, for she was not hidden very well. As soon as it was safe to venture out, she set her horse at a gallop; she wanted to get off the highway as quickly as possible.

But wood paths did not prove very safe either. It was towards evening when, having halted by a creek, Emily heard voices in the woods. Swiftly she turned her horse and sought a good hiding place in the underbrush. From it she peered through the foliage, her heart berating a tattoo. Who were these men? Friends or foes? And where were they going?

She did not have to wait long. A band of Tories on foot pushed through the bushes and stopped at the creek. How fortunate it was, Emily reflected, she had gone off the path to drink and water her horse!

"Let's see if we find tracks around here," said one of the men, and Emily caught her breath.

"'Twould be a waste of time," said another. "If anyone had passed here we'd have met him; it's the only path in this wilderness."

"Come on, 'tis getting dark," said a third and they went on.

As Emily emerged from her hiding place, she noted that it was getting dark. Her horse was tired. She would have to spend the night somewhere. But where? She knew that the path she was on led to a settlement. But she also knew that most of its inhabitants were Tories, and she must not risk going there.

After some deliberation Emily decided to make a wide detour and stop at some farmhouse, far beyond the settlement.

The stars were out and the warm summer night had settled on the countryside when Emily at last sighted a house. She was so tired and hungry by then that she did not even stop to wonder who lived there, but rode straight to the house.

An elderly farmer came to the door.

"I am Emily Geiger," she told him. "I am on my way to the Elwood farm, but I'm too tired to go on. Can you put me up?"

"Are you John Geiger's daughter?"

"Yes."

"Well, I know and like your father, even though he is a Whig," said the farmer. "'Twill be a pleasure to serve his daughter."

"We'd give you food and shelter even if you were the daughter of our worst enemy," said the farmer's wife, who had joined her husband at the door.

Well, they had treated her as if she were the daughter of their best friend, Emily reflected, when, after eating a good supper, she was shown to her room. And she had told them that when she thanked them. But she had refused to have breakfast in the morning. "Abby's waiting for me," she had told the farmer's wife, bidding her good night.

Emily had made up her mind to sleep only a few hours and ride away at daybreak. She knew that roads were not as well patrolled during the night, and she wanted to take advantage of it. Therefore she only took off her bonnet and her shoes and threw herself upon the bed. She was asleep as soon her head touched the pillow.

It was shortly after midnight that her slumber came to an abrupt end. She sat up with a jerk. What had awakened her? The sound of a galloping horse. Nonsense, she must have dreamt it. She listened. A horse was running along the road, coming nearer and nearer. Had she been seen and traced here? She decided she must leave at once!

She hastily tied her bonnet and, carrying her shoes in her hand, crept to the window.

The night was clear and Emily, watching the road, was able to discern the silhouette of a horseman. Was he going to pass by? No, he turned off the road; he was coming to the door. As Emily bent down to put on her shoes she heard him stop and call: "Night patrol! Anything suspicious?"

Then a window was raised and the farmer replied: "That you, Joe? Come in and have some beer."

It was time to go, Emily thought. The farmer might not even mention her presence, but she was not taking any chances! She climbed out of the window and walked stealthily to the stable. As she drew near it a dog came sniffing at her. She quickly bent down and spoke softly to him, scratching behind his ear, and he licked her hand.

To saddle the horse and lead him out was the work of a moment. And in another Emily was riding through the fields to deaden the sound of the hoofs.

Dawn was breaking when she finally reached the woods. She slowed down and listened. No suspicious noise ruffled the stillness around her. She was safe. And she might just as well be on her way, she decided, for who knew what delays she might encounter later on. But luck seemed to be with her, so much so that towards noon Emily relaxed her watchfulness and let her thoughts drift to other subjects. She thought of her father. How worried he must be! She'd have to send word to him immediately upon reaching Abby's home. She would be there in a couple of hours. She would have something to eat, for she was ravenous already, and then Abby's husband would take her to see Sumter . . . and her mission would be fulfilled. It had been easy, even too easy, and not dangerous at all. One had only to know paths and trails, and for her, who had roamed this wilderness since she could hold onto a horse....

"Halt!" cried a voice.

Emily was so startled that she almost lost her balance. She steadied herself and looked up. A party of British scouts was barring the road. She saw at once that she was caught and she sat still, waiting for the ordeal.

Questions were hurled at her in such quick succession and with such an evident purpose of confusing her that Emily was disconcerted, blushed, began to stammer.

This confirmed the scouts in their worst suspicions and, after a short conference among themselves, they decided to take their prisoner to the nearest farmhouse and have her searched by the farmer's wife.

Emily was crestfallen. It was all her own fault. How stupid of her to feel safe before reaching her destination. Then also, after all the rehearsing she had done for just such an occasion, to get confused, and worse still, to blush and to stammer! What was going to happen now? She had no fear for herself; her chief concern was to get released and to proceed on her way. To this end she should first destroy the letter. But how? This was not the first time she had asked herself this question and the answer had always been the same—she'll have to eat it! And next she'll have to pretend to be a halfwit, to justify her conduct of a moment ago.

By the time their party came to a farmhouse Emily was ready for action. The scouts locked her in a room and the officers went in search of the farmer's wife. No sooner had the key turned in the lock than Emily had the letter in her hands and was tearing it into small fragments. Then she began eating them. But they were dry and, as her throat was parched, the process of chewing was a hard one. She almost choked each time she swallowed a piece. And time pressed; she could hear the voices of the British officer and of the matron coming nearer and nearer. The door was opening when Emily stuffed the last two fragments into her mouth. She tried to swallow them in a hurry but they scratched her throat and stuck there. As a last resort she covered her face with her hands and burst into convulsive sobs.

"There, there," said the farmer's wife, who was softhearted, "there's nothing to weep about."

Emily swallowed hard—thank God she had done it—and lifted her tear-stained face to the matron.

"Come on," continued the good woman. "Take off your things. I just want to see if you are concealing anything. . . ."

"Concealing!" Emily cried, bursting into fresh sobs. "But that's wicked . . . and I'm not wicked . . . I've done nothing . . . nothing at all! I was only going to see Abby . . . and her new baby . . . Abby's my best friend . . . I . . . I . . ." and she sobbed as though her heart would break.

The matron was convinced of Emily's innocence. She patted her on the shoulder and went out muttering about the dumbness of men who would suspect even such a guileless child.

She must have told the scouts just what she thought of them, Emily decided, for the officer was quite red in the face when he came to tell her she was free to continue her journey.

Emily jumped into the saddle and rode straight to Abby's home. And she insisted that her friend's husband take her at once to General Sumter.

Excitement flared high in Sumter's camp when the news spread that a messenger from General Greene had broken through and that the messenger was a girl still in her teens.

General Sumter received Emily at once, and she repeated word by word the message contained in the letter she had had such a difficult time swallowing.

"South Carolina will never forget the debt of gratitude she owes you," declared Sumter and extended to Emily the hospitality of his camp.

But Emily declined with thanks. She wanted to visit with Abby and then hurry home, for her father needed her.

◊◊◊

$\mathcal{L}$ittle **RHODY**

Charles Newton Hood

Well over a hundred years ago, during the 1890s, this story took place. Horses, so soon to be displaced by automobiles, still ruled supreme. But even so, few city girls knew how to handle them.

Of the thirteen girls chosen to represent the thirteen original colonies, "Little Rhody" was the most unlikely to have been chosen, had but recently moved there, and had few friends.

But all that was before the big Memorial Day parade. . . .

There was on the big Memorial Day poster one announcement that caused a flutter among the schoolgirls of Washington village, and thus it ran:

> THE GRAVES OF THE FALLEN HEROES WILL
> BE ADORNED WITH FLORAL TRIBUTES BY
> THIRTEEN CHOSEN YOUNG LADIES,
> IN COSTUME, REPRESENTING THE
> THIRTEEN ORIGINAL STATES.

And the "thirteen chosen young ladies" had not, as yet, been selected, the committee deeming the engagement of the band and speakers, the raising of the necessary funds for the expenses of the day, the soliciting of flowers, and the preparations for the grand parade of far greater importance. So, indeed, they were; but meantime the anxious hearts of the fifty-two young ladies in the Washington Village Union Free School beat impatiently.

Perhaps the members of the committee had become a trifle appalled at the problem that confronted them in the selection. It had seemed all easy enough when the plan was formulated, but so many hints had been given to them respecting their selection by fond mothers and brothers and fathers of willing representatives of original commonwealths that the "prominent young businessmen" who composed the committee, and who desired to offend nobody, after several fruitless meetings were almost in despair.

It had been intended, at first, to have all of the states represented; but the Union had grown so large that this plan seemed impracticable. Then the plan of having only the northern states represented was discussed; but this idea was promptly voted down as not carrying out the "no North, no South" ideal of the present generation, in the letter as well as in the spirit.

Then the idea of having only twenty of the larger states represented was discussed; but, as the chairman said, "Washington Village desires to slight no commonwealth in our glorious Union"; and it was at length decided, as by all odds the best solution of the problem, to have only the thirteen original states represented, just as on the Fourth of July.

Then followed the difficulty of selection. A bright member of the committee finally saw a little light, and suggested that only daughters of soldiers be eligible. So with this decision the committee tramped up to the Washington Village Union Free School, and made known their errand to the principal.

It was quickly found that the "daughters of soldiers" idea made the task of selection very easy, for the principal could recall but ten of his pupils who were eligible. These ten accepted at once and with pride.

The principal, addressing the school, asked if there were not some other young ladies who were daughters of soldiers, and two more girls arose and proved their claim to the honor.

"We need only one more," remarked the principal. "Is there any other young lady in the school who is a daughter of a soldier of the Civil War?"

And then the new scholar, Rhoda Ireland, rose timidly to her feet. "I am, sir," she said.

The principal looked puzzled. No one knew much about the new girl. She was an orphan who had come from somewhere in the West only the week before, and she was living with an aunt in Washington Village.

"Can you tell us, Rhoda," asked the principal, "your father's regiment?"

"Yes, sir," replied the little girl. "He was in the Twelfth Alabama Cavalry."

The principal turned red, cleared his throat, and looked helplessly toward the committee. Two or three of the girls giggled in that nervous, mirthless, senseless, meaningless way that some schoolgirls have, and the new girl understood in a moment. Her eyes filled with tears, and her lip trembled, but she stood her ground.

Then it was that the young businessman who was chairman of the Memorial Day committee proved his right to the position by stepping quickly down from the rostrum, walking over to the little girl, and grasping her hand.

"Thank you, little one," he said. "We're proud to have you take part with us. I've heard of the Twelfth Alabamas, and they were brave men, every one."

And so the question was decided, and many meetings of the "thirteen chosen young ladies" were held to discuss the plan and costumes for the day.

Although the dresses of the girls were to be practically all alike, each daughter of a soldier chose a state to represent; and the little western girl, partly on account of her size, and partly on account of her name, was assigned Rhode Island, and promptly nicknamed "Little Rhody."

She became something of a favorite at once and would have been much more popular had she not been so shy and reserved and also if it had not been for the almost universal custom of schoolgirls in their teens to have always one and only *one* dearest girl friend and chum at a time; and in a company of thirteen girls there was bound to be an odd one; so Little Rhody did most of her discussing about her costume with her aunt, and felt proud but lonely.

It is so pleasant to write a tale without any "villain" or mean person in it, and there wasn't one of those twelve other girls who was not as sweet and nice and good as any girls that you ever knew or read about; and if they were not as cordial and chummy with Little Rhody as they might have been, it was thoughtlessness and nothing more.

When the thirteen girls were dressed in their pretty costumes on Memorial Day afternoon, they presented indeed a fascinating spectacle. Their dresses were of gauzy white, their sashes of brightest red, and their

Goddess of Liberty caps of deepest blue spangled with gilt stars. They looked like patriotic fairies. At one o'clock they met at the school building.

All day long the little village had been filling with country visitors, and the streets were crowded. Bunting and flags and flowers were everywhere, and detached members of various civic and military organizations, in full uniform, were hurrying importantly through the throng.

The president of the day, a very pale little man, who sat up very straight on an exceedingly large, black horse, rode frequently down the street and back again, apparently with no definite object, but seemingly much burdened with his responsibility; and two open carriages, which were to convey to the cemetery the village officers, the clergy, and speakers of the day, were standing in front of the leading hotel.

Up somewhere in one of the buildings, the Washington Village Silver Cornet Band could be heard putting the finishing touches of rehearsal on "The Star-Spangled Banner" and "The Red, White, and Blue."

The "thirteen chosen young ladies . . . representing the thirteen original states," gathered in a picturesque group on the schoolhouse steps, voiced a united "Oh!" of delight as four beautiful gray horses, with plumes in their bridles and with flower-trimmed harnesses, pranced proudly around the corner and then came to a stop directly in front of the school building.

The fine four-in-hand was attached to the gorgeous bandwagon owned by the Washington Village Palace Livery, and the proprietor of the Washington Village Palace Livery himself sat upon the driver's seat and handled the reins.

The procession was to move promptly at two o'clock, and was to form "at half past one, sharp, upon Eagle Street, with the right resting on Main." It was now twenty-five minutes after one, and the proprietor of the Washington Village Palace Livery, who prided himself greatly on always being on time, or a little previous, urged the girls to "climb in lively, for the people down street is all waitin' to see you!"

The young ladies accordingly scrambled into the wagon as rapidly as possible. Now, the bandwagon had three double seats, each accommodating four persons, two of whom faced forward and two backward, and there was one small extra seat in the extreme front. The driver's seat was high above the rest, and on each side of it and extending back were highly gilded, carved figures representing savage dragons, so that the little extra seat was a very inconspicuous one indeed. How it happened no one of the girls, or her chum, could have told; there was nothing premeditated about it; but when Little Rhody finally got into the wagon, all of the seats were fully occupied, except the small one hidden away between the dragons.

As the equipage moved slowly down the street to reach the starting point of the parade, it attracted a great deal of attention from people who were hurrying toward the main street to see the procession, or toward the cemetery a mile away to hear the exercises. Had one taken the trouble to count the fair representatives of the States, he would have had trouble discovering more than a dozen, for only the tip of Rhoda's cap was visible above the dragons. But Rhoda didn't mind. She knew scarcely anyone, anyway, and she was so modest and shy that she was half glad that she did not have a more prominent place.

As it happened, however—but we will tell the story in proper order.

"Well, we're the only ones on time," remarked the jovial driver, as the vehicle turned into Eagle Street, where the only portion of the procession waiting was the "flower wagon," loaded down with tier upon tier of beautiful bouquets in solid banks, wreaths, baskets, and floral designs, and with every portion of the wheels and body of the wagon concealed by trimmings of flowers, vines, and evergreens, while floral blankets covered the horses, and a canopy of evergreens over the wagon sheltered the flowers from the direct rays of the sun.

Near the head of the street, the "Chariot of the States" was drawn up on one side of the roadway, just ahead of the flower wagon; for the "thirteen chosen young ladies" were to have the place of honor, third in the line, preceded only by the president of the day and his assistants on horseback, the officers of the village, ministers, orator, and poet in carriages, the Thirty-ninth Separate Company National Guards of the State, and the Washington Village Silver Cornet Band.

As always with processions, this one was late in starting. The hot May sun beat down stiflingly upon the girls in the uncovered bandwagon; but to little Rhody, fresh from the extreme temperatures of New Mexico, it seemed like only a pleasant, sunshiny day.

"I wish that we could have brought our parasols," sighed Pennsylvania, a very stout girl, as she violently fanned her flushed face with her handkerchief. "Just look at Rhoda Ireland, girls. Why, Rhody, you don't look as if you minded it at all!"

"I don't, much," said Rhoda. "I've been used to living where it is pretty hot nearly all of the time."

Just then the driver, who had been grumbling loudly for ten minutes about people who were never on time, noticed a strap in the harness of the "nigh" wheelhorse which was incorrectly adjusted, and laying the four reins carefully over the back of his high seat, and looking over at Rhoda, he said, "Jest hold the ends of them lines a minute, little girl," clambered down the side of the wagon, and began the readjustment of the offending strap.

"Oh, Mr. Colt," exclaimed North Carolina, nervously, "isn't it dangerous to leave the horses like that? Suppose they should start?"

"I'd catch 'em," replied the driver, as with head down he struggled with the harness. "And besides, they won't start. Oh, them hosses ain't afraid of nothin'. Why, I could drive them hosses right up to an *en*-jine, an' they'd eat oats off it. I—*whoa!* WHOA!"

For at this moment the Thirty-ninth Separate Company National Guards rounded the corner just back of the wagon, and the band struck up a lively air. The horses, who were used to bands, though the music always made them a trifle nervous, would have been all right, except that the very instant after the music struck up, an innocent little bit of paper, floating on a gentle breeze, flapped lazily into the view of the "off" leader.

Coming just at the moment when the off leader had not fully decided whether the band was the usual thing and perfectly safe or not, it startled the animal, and he gave a quick little jump. This alarmed the three other horses, already nervous, and they all moved forward a few steps very quickly—so quickly that the fat proprietor of the Palace Livery Stable was tumbled heels over head against the curbstone. The horses trotted along a few steps. Six or seven of the states shrieked in concert. The new drum corps of the Washington Village Cadets turned in from another street, and the horses hurried along a little faster. Then, not feeling the hard pull on the reins and the reassuring voice of their driver, they lost their heads entirely, made up their minds that something dreadful was coming behind them, broke into a wild run, and rounded the corner into Main Street at a speed which almost tipped over the clumsy vehicle.

The frightened girls clung together, shrieking wildly.

"Stop that noise, girls!" Little Rhody, timid and abashed no longer, was standing up in the bounding, swaying chariot, and was speaking in a tone of command. "Keep still; you'll frighten them more. Hang on tight, now, and don't any of you dare try to jump!" she cried, as she placed one foot on the back of one of the dragons, and, hanging tightly to the four reins, climbed over onto the high driver's seat, just as the four maddened animals straightened out into the main street.

A brave man in a veteran's uniform made a dash at the heads of the leaders, but was thrown down.

Calmly, and without pulling a particle, Little Rhody was arranging the reins in her hands, just as her father had taught her on the box of the Santa Fe stagecoach when she took her regular fortnightly trip with him so that the best driver of the route could keep acquainted with his little girl; and even in the peril of the moment she remembered how he used to let her get the reins all nicely adjusted, and then yell at the six mules until they were running like mad, laugh at her good-naturedly as she struggled to pull them down, and pat her on the back and tell her that she was her father's own girl when she handled the team nicely.

She was all alone now, and the chances were desperate, but she must do the best that she could.

Slowly, and without a word to startle the horses afresh with a strange voice, she settled back on the reins with a steady pull.

They'll probably run straight, she thought, *until we come to the turn that goes to the stable.*

"If you can't stop 'em," her father had said, "don't try. Keep 'em in the road and tire 'em out."

And Little Rhody couldn't stop them.

The great animals, with ears back and necks outstretched, with terror-stricken eyes and dilated nostrils, were hurling forward with maddened bounds, dragging the great, thundering, clattering chariot after them with terrific speed.

It was the residence portion now, and the thoroughfare was comparatively clear; but on ahead the crowded business section was growing nearer and nearer.

The Washington Village Independent Fire Engine Company, marching up the street in their new red shirts, were met and scattered like a flock of sheep.

A shout of horror went up from the throats of the hundreds of people who lined the sidewalks, aghast at the prospect, yet powerless to help. Horses and carriages were hurried out of the way; but the streets were so crowded that a terrible catastrophe seemed imminent.

A clumsy driver, in his haste to escape, backed his wagon directly across the way, and in an instant it was struck by the heavy chariot and smashed to kindling wood.

The rushing horses veered a little to the left, and missed, by a hairsbreadth almost, a carriage filled with ladies and children. Unconsciously the animals were beginning to follow somewhat the guidance of the little girl who, with her gaudy liberty cap blown back and her black hair streaming, stood, braced backward on the footboard, pulling desperately upon the reins.

Again the horses sheered slightly to the right, and the great crashing wheels only brushed the mass of people crowded out into the street at a crossing, and yet left unharmed the baby carriage abandoned by a frightened nurse in the middle of the street. It was marvelous.

Now they were approaching the turn which led to the right, down a steep alley, to the Palace Stables. Beyond the turn Main Street was straight and clear. Could she get the horses by? They were already veering toward the awful turn. The prospect was frightful.

Little Rhody, pale as death, and with teeth hard set, waited until the noses of the leaders were directly opposite the alley, and then, throwing all of her strength into a pull on the left-hand reins, she yelled at the horses again and again that old, free, wild yell of the stagecoach days.

For a tiny instant, puzzled and startled by this new, strange voice, the horses forgot for a single moment their insane desire to turn that home corner, and in that instant the brave little driver prevailed.

With a wide half-circle which carried the chariot up onto the alley crossing and back into the street again, they were past that danger and away again.

"Now let 'em run!" muttered the little girl, repeating the words of her father; and run they did, straight down the center of the wide, smooth, clear street, like a stampede of wild horses, over the stone bridge and out on the north road, without slackening speed, guided by that firm pair of little hands.

Country people, driving in to see the parade, crowded their horses and wagons close against the fences to get out of the way. Plucky young farmers rushed out into the road ahead of the flying horses, but drew back, knowing that their efforts would be futile.

Half a mile out, the horses began to tire a bit, and lagged a trifle; and then little Rhoda, fearing to have them stop while still comparatively fresh, actually urged them on to speed again, until, three quarters of the way up Cemetery Hill, they finally dropped into a trot, then into a walk, and finally into an exhausted tug up the remainder of the ascent.

The soldiers' plot in the cemetery was crowded with people awaiting the arrival of the procession and the beginning of the exercises; and a dozen men sprang to the heads of the reeking, panting, subdued, but nervous horses; while "twelve chosen young ladies," representing twelve of the original states, tumbled, helter-skelter, out of the chariot.

But poor, overwrought Little Rhody, now that the danger was past, collapsed into a trembling little red, white, and blue heap on the footboard, and buried her face in the cushions of the high driver's seat, sobbing hysterically.

By and by the people began to catch up, the proprietor of the Palace Livery Stable ahead, in the flower wagon, driving at a breakneck pace; then the president of the day on his big black horse, with his assistants close behind; and then everybody who had horses to drive; and finally the procession itself, very much disorganized and blown from much double-quicking—the Washington Village Silver Cornet Band, the Thirty-ninth Separate Company National Guards, the Independent Fire Engine Company, the Washington Village Cadets, the sons of veterans, the veterans themselves, the civic societies, and the village officers, clergy, poet, and orator in carriages.

And everybody said that what Little Rhody had done was wonderful; and they made much of the little lady, who was once more a shy, modest, retiring little girl, that for a long time the exercises could not be begun at all; and when they began, the president of the day made Rhoda, in spite of her protests, come up and sit beside him in the front row on the platform,

where everybody could see her; and once, when the speaker of the day
compared the bravery of Little Rhody with the bravery of a soldier on
the field of battle, the throng cheered and shouted and yelled so loud and
long that the band had to break in and play "The Star-Spangled Banner"
through three times before the orator could go on.

◊◊◊

Rich but
NOT GAUDY

Ruth Orendorff

Oh no! Her dear friend Bonny Rae was descending on the ranch at the very worst time. Last visit she'd left the place in a shambles, shampooing pigs and putting permanents in their tails; and applying so much bleach on her freckled brother's face that most of his facial skin peeled off!

And Dad trusted her to make that important horse sale while he was gone. What if Bonny Rae wrecked that too?

Leitha Crawford was perched on top of a manger in the warm, shadowy barn fragrant with the scent of hay, murmurous with the munching of the cows and the gentle snorts of the horses in the stalls. Her brown hands were clasped over her knees, and she was chewing a straw absently as she listened to her brother.

"Either way you look at it, it should be worth the trip." Garth was arguing as much to convince himself as his sister. "If the horses don't take any ribbons, at least I shall have had a chance to show our stuff and maybe make a sale. With Dad's rheumatism and all, we could use the money."

"Could we!" Leitha interjected fervently.

"If you're sure you can swing it here, Leitha—"

"Why not? Haven't I helped around the barn ever since I could reach as high as a horse's head? And Roddy will help a lot."

He looked around doubtfully. "Well, it's quite a change from writing poetry and translating French to milking cows and grooming horses."

"Not to mention cleaning the barn," she giggled. "I'm going to like it, so it's decided."

She slid down from the manger and went out into the winter sunlight. It was mail time.

If she could have known what lay in the mailbox as she skipped blithely down the driveway, her hands thrust deep in her overalls pockets, her whistle would not have been so carefree.

She reached for the daily paper and drew out with it a square pink envelope scented with gardenia. Bonny Rae Gordon. It couldn't be anybody else. She ripped open the envelope eagerly; Bonny Rae had been one of her very best friends during those four high school years just ended with the midwinter graduation.

As Bonny Rae's big careless scrawl became intelligible, she felt herself stiffening with dismay.

"Tuesday," Leitha murmured under her breath. "Tomorrow—and Garth will be getting off to the horse show in the morning." She felt a little panicky. Garth would never go if he knew that Bonny Rae was coming, on top of the burden of work and responsibility already shifting onto her shoulders. She decided not to tell him; not to tell *anyone.*

But eight-year-old Roddy smelled the gardenia and recognized the pink envelope. "Bonny Rae coming?" he shrilled with fatal perception.

"Bonny Rae?" Garth was at the table. "She's coming? Then the show's off. I'm staying here. No telling what I'd find when I came back. Remember how she practically tore the place to pieces last time with her crazy ideas of shampooing the pigs and putting permanents in their tails?"

"She's more sensible now," Leitha assured him.

"Still bent on being a beauty shop operator and practicing on everybody and everything she sees?" Garth persisted relentlessly.

"I—I'm afraid so," Leitha faltered. "But, Garth, you're not going to back out on her account."

"Remember when she tried to bleach Roddy's freckles and took most of the skin off his face?"

"She's specializing on hair and manicuring now," Leitha pleaded.

It was a hard job but she finally got Garth off, still uneasy and suspicious of the coming guest. She welcomed Bonny Rae, and her heart melted again as it always did when her pretty, flighty guest was effusively glad to see her and thrilled at the prospect of helping her care for things during Garth's absence.

It was Bonny Rae who woke her that night after she had drifted off to sleep. "It's Garth on the telephone," she whispered, her blue eyes looking big and dark in her small pointed face. She was bending over Leitha's bed with a big flashlight gripped tightly in her hand. "He sounds excited. Oh, do hurry, Leitha."

Leitha raced down to the phone in the hall.

"That you, Leitha?" Garth's eager voice came over the wire. "Hope I didn't scare you, but night rates are cheaper, you know. Don't be surprised if somebody comes out to look at the horses. I'm telling you so you'll have things in shape. Two or three men have talked to me already. They liked Sea Breeze. Everything okay so far? Bonny Rae up to anything? Well, so long."

She padded back up the stairs. "He just wants me to keep everything shipshape for buyers," she explained to her anxious guest. "Just as if I wouldn't, anyway. Come on, let's get back into bed. I'll have to roll out at six tomorrow to milk those cows."

"Six?" Bonnie Rae wailed. "Why don't we just stay up?"

But at six Bonny Rae got up too and followed Leitha along the trodden snow path to the barn. She tried to help milk, laughing at her own efforts.

"Ooh, what a little beauty," she squealed, catching sight of thoroughbred Sea Breeze's youngest colt. "That silvery mane looks like foam curling up over his shoulder. And his darling bushy tail is going to be just like it."

"Just like his mother," Leitha said. "We were disappointed that Tradewind didn't inherit that silvery mane and tail too." She added gallantly. "But we love him just the same." She reached over the box stall to pat the tall three-year-old's sleek sorrel flank. "See how gentle he is."

Bonny Rae got on well with Roddy in spite of the disastrous attempt to eliminate his freckles, now thicker than ever. Before morning turned to noon he was showing her afresh all over the place and swelling importantly as he dispensed information right and left.

All in all, Leitha told herself as she brushed her hair at bedtime, the day had passed as slick as sliding down a greased pole.

In the morning she hummed blithely as she dressed, secure in the comfortable feeling that everything was going well and that Garth would feel proud of her when he came back. That was why it was all the more numbing to get the bad news at breakfast.

Mrs. Crawford turned troubled eyes on her daughter as she brought in a bowl of hot cereal. "I'm glad Bonny Rae isn't up yet, Leitha," she said. "There's something I must tell you. The mare is gone."

"Gone," Leitha repeated. "You mean she got out?"

"The barn door was open and so was the door to her stall when Roddy went out there first thing this morning. Surely you were not that careless?"

Neither had heard the footsteps coming into the room. The first hint either had of Bonny Rae's presence was a quick indrawn breath behind them. Leitha whirled round quickly to confront her guest. Bonny Rae's lips were quivering and her blue eyes were wide with fright.

"I did it," she wailed. "I just had to slip out after supper to see if the horses would take sugar from my hand the way Roddy said they would. The catch on Kitty's stall was hard to fasten, but I thought I got it shut safely. I—I must not have."

"But the barn door," Leitha said. "It was open or the mare could not have gotten out."

"I–I know," Bonny Rae faltered. "I couldn't shut it. It stuck. I meant to tell you. I must have forgotten."

"It's my fault really," Leitha offered generously. "I should have gone out to the barn last thing before I went to bed to see that everything was okay. Garth always does that. And don't you worry about Kitty. Since I know that she walked out of her own accord, I could take you to her with my eyes shut."

"The Branfield pasture?" Mrs. Crawford hazarded.

"Exactly." Leitha nodded confidently. "She's spent every summer there for several years," she explained to Bonny Rae. "She's sure to be there."

"I'll go with you," Bonny Rae offered eagerly.

"You will not," Leitha declared sternly. "Don't you hear that wind howling and see that snow flying about? No delicate city orchid is going out there with me this morning."

"I'll make it up to you," Bonny Rae vowed penitently.

Well started on her search for the straying mare, Leitha was glad she had discouraged Bonny Rae from coming, and before she reached home she was supremely thankful. In the first place the mare was not in the Branfield pasture. The wind had blown tracks, if any, full of snow; and after an hour's search Leitha could not tell whether the mare had ever been there.

She was near exhaustion when she gave up hope and tramped to the Branfield farmhouse to rest. She had lunch there. Mr. Branfield was driving to town and wanted to take her home on his way, but she refused. By that time the wind was gone and the snow lay in a still, glittering blanket. She was eager to begin the search again.

Again she found no tracks. She wandered aimlessly, frequently stopping at farmhouses to inquire if Kitty had been seen.

"No," she heard at the last one, "but there's a call for you from your home."

"Where have you been?" her mother's voice came over the wire when she called home. "We've been trying to get in touch with you for hours. Kitty is back. She came in around noon. Roddy's done his best to give her a rubdown. He and Bonny Rae have been at the barn almost all day. You'd better rest before you come home, but I did want you to know about Kitty."

Relieved, Leitha stayed to rest awhile before she set out on the three-mile tramp that lay between her and home. It was after three o'clock when she turned into the driveway.

Bonny Rae, eyes sparkling, ran out to meet her. "Everything's okay," she called triumphantly. "Roddy and I took good care of Kitty when she came home, and we've a marvelous surprise for you."

A cold shiver of apprehension ran over Leitha. Bonny Rae tugged at her arm, leading her toward the barn.

She stopped at Tradewind's roomy stall. "There," she exclaimed complacently. "What do you think of it?"

Leitha glanced obediently toward the colt. "Why—why, that isn't Tradewind." Her jaw dropped helplessly, her eyes slowly filled with dismay. "What in the world have you done to him?" She leaned over to touch him, to run her fingers along his mane. She had left Tradewind a solid sorrel color, without mark or blemish. She found him now with a pale, flowing tail and a fringe of straw-colored mane.

"Bonny Rae, whatever have you done?" she moaned.

Bonny Rae looked first incredulous, then frightened. "I—I was sure you would like it. Don't you remember, you said only yesterday all of you were so disappointed because he wasn't marked like his mother?"

"Ah, he looks swell," Roddy declared stoutly. "We worked almost all day over him."

They had done it with peroxide, it developed, Bonny Rae putting into practice some of her new beauty lore. They had used all the Crawford supply of peroxide, and Roddy had borrowed from neighbors. Tradewind had behaved beautifully while the bleaching was going on. Both boy and girl were hurt and surprised at Leitha's reaction.

Leitha felt like shaking her, but she refrained. *What would Garth say?* she kept thinking over and over.

So much depended on a sale, especially since her father's doctor bills were mounting. She tried to control her feelings, to keep from Bonny Rae just how tragic her well-meant effort might turn out. *For nobody,* Leitha thought dully, *would ever buy Tradewind with that bleached mane and tail.*

"No use crying over spilled oats, as Dad says," she said as lightly as she could. "Let's all pitch in and get this barn into shape. It is a mess."

"Someone's coming," Roddy shouted from the doorway. "In a big shiny car."

Leitha paled and leaned hard on her stable fork. A buyer—and the barn was a mess. Tradewind was practically ruined.

The man was a buyer all right, and he wanted to look at Sea Breeze's colt.

"My daughter greatly admired the mare your brother has with him in the city," he said. "That sorrel with the silvery mane and tail took her fancy. She wants something just like that. I don't care much about color, but you know how girls are. If the colt is as sound and gentle as your brother claims and takes after his mother in color, I think we have only to settle on the price."

"B-but he's—" Leitha stammered in bewilderment and stopped. Was the man getting Tradewind mixed with the baby foal? She moved toward its stall.

"Here's Sea Breeze's foal," she said. "We have a three-year-old, but he's a uniform sorrel from his muzzle to the tip of his tail."

The man looked in bewilderment from the little colt to Leitha.

"Gwen must have been confused," he said finally, chuckling at the cocky little foal. "She wants to ride the horse, not make a lap dog out of it. Well, let's see the three-year-old sorrel. More to my taste. 'Rich but not gaudy,' that's my motto." He marched straight for Tradewind's stall and stopped short. "Hold on, what's this? This is what Gwen wants."

Silence fell over the others in the stable. Leitha tried to moisten dry lips but words would not come. If she just kept still now, if the others would only keep still—but she could not. No Crawford could. Square dealing was the Crawford motto.

The man did not look disgusted or disappointed after she told him. He threw back his head and laughed while Bonny Rae's cheeks got redder than any rouge could make them. Finally he sobered. "Sure that'll grow in sorrel again? You'll guarantee that? Okay, if his gaits are right I'll take him. Sorrel's my color. No flashy stuff for me. And Gwen will be tickled with that silver mane and tail. By the time it's gone she'll love the colt so much she won't mind the difference."

"But you'll tell her?" Leitha pleaded. "You won't—"

"Sa-ay," the man protested in mock indignation. "Think a Crawford can beat me in square dealing?"

With the check in her hand Leitha watched him drive away before she turned jubilantly to Bonny Rae. "You did it, Bonny Rae. You really made the sale."

"No, I didn't," Bonny Rae disclaimed. "No more meddling from me. 'Rich but not gaudy'—that's my motto from now on. And you can tell Garth so."

◆◆◆

A Satisfactory
INVESTMENT

Eveline W. Brainerd

Great-aunt Eunice, in her annual visit to the Kelsey Farm, concluded that it was time to try an experiment with her thirteen-year-old grandniece: Was she really capable of spending money wisely? She decided to risk five dollars (a large sum of money back when this story was written) on little Prudence, in order to find out.

It certainly didn't look like she'd made a wise investment.

Prudence sat in a little runabout before the village store waiting for her father. Buying paint had proved a slow proceeding, and she wished he had fastened the horse so that she might go in and see what there was new in ginghams and ribbons. She put her hand in her pocket to be sure that her little purse was safe. She wanted to take it out to assure herself that nothing had happened to the crisp five-dollar bill, but that was too childish for her thirteen years, and she contented herself with pinching the leather now and then and fancying that she felt the paper crackle.

Great-aunt Eunice Spencer, who had just gone, after her annual visit to the farm, had made her grandniece this extraordinary gift the evening before her departure.

"We'll put it in the bank the next time we go to Deep Water," said Mrs. Kelsey, smiling at her daughter's astonished silence. "You've never had as much as that to deposit at once, have you, Prudence?"

"No, we won't, Nancy," interfered Aunt Eunice, genially. "Prudence is to spend that money just as she chooses."

The girl's eyes grew round with astonishment. Spend five dollars! She had spent four last year on materials for Christmas gifts for the entire family. These purchases, however, had stretched over six months, as opportunities came for dropping corn, or weeding the cold-frames, or gathering berries. But here was five dollars, all at once, and not destined, a penny of it, for that highly respectable but all-devouring and unresponsive bank.

When she had gone to bed, Aunt Eunice, who was by no means as old as great-aunts are supposed to be, laughed. Her niece, Nancy, not much younger, shook her head.

"It has to be as you say, of course, but spendthrifts are so common nowadays that we don't believe in much money for Prudence."

"No more do I," Miss Spencer returned. "I don't recall giving her any before. You've been training her some years. Now I'm curious to see what she'll do when left to herself. I'm curious five dollars' worth."

So it came about that no one offered advice. No one even inquired how Prudence was planning to use her fortune. She had suddenly achieved independence, and knew how her brother had felt on his twenty-first birthday.

It was, after all, better that her father had not fastened the horse, she reflected as she sat in the runabout. If she should see Mr. Wells's autumn stock, she might be tempted to an unconsidered purchase. Her eyes searched the road for amusement. Just then, around the corner swung an odd procession. Several large covered wagons, each with a driver apparently asleep, came first. Behind were smaller, box-like affairs, with canvas about their sides. These were drawn by eight Shetland ponies, while a hound, as large as they, stalked beside, and an Irish terrier with matted hair trotted near. A huge chariot, whose tarnished gilding showed through the tattered wrappings, followed, and behind stumbled a tall, gaunt, black horse. The whole outfit showed dingy and disheveled in the bright morning. Every driver was lying across his seat, or back on his load, and seemed only awake enough to shout "Get up!" now and again to his plodding team. The animals were unkempt and thin, but the black horse was the thinnest of all. Prudence turned in the seat, and, leaning her chin against the back, gazed after him.

"Oh-h!" she said pityingly, as he stumbled.

"Circus?" inquired Mr. Kelsey, as he came out bearing two gallon cans.

"Yes. Is it going to be here?" demanded Prudence with interest.

"Guess not. Going on to Deep Water for tonight. Did you think you'd take us all with your money?"

Prudence shook her head.

"It didn't look very interesting. Do you suppose there were really wild animals in the small wagons? I saw bars on one where the canvas fell down."

"Oh, they'd manage to get a secondhand lion or tiger, anyway. It wouldn't be a circus without a lion."

"I know the horses are hungry. There's a dear black one just starved."

Mr. Wells, coming with more cans, glanced down the road.

"I hope the cages are strong if they give the tiger as little as they give the dogs," he said. "Must have been a bad season. They all looked as though they'd forgotten the taste of a square meal."

"There, that'll do," said Mr. Kelsey, tucking a horse blanket about his purchases to keep them from rattling. "Now, Prue, if you don't want to do any more trading—" and his pleasant eyes seemed to smile at her.

"No," she replied seriously, "I'm not going to buy anything now." She barely saved herself from saying "here," which might have hurt Mr. Wells's feelings.

"Start along then." Her father swung himself to the seat beside her, and she started the pretty brown horse on toward the blacksmith's shop. When the errands were done, and, toward noon, they neared Hillside Farm, there in the little locust grove at the bend of the road by their orchard was the circus cavalcade.

"Sure enough, they are thin!" commented Mr. Kelsey. "Careful as you swing in, Prudence. Don't hit a wheel." Prudence steered the glossy, well-fed Moses between the posts and drew up at the carriage-house door.

"Good!" said her father, approvingly. "You drive pretty well, now. Let's unharness and give the pony his dinner. I have to use him all afternoon."

Prudence on one side and her father on the other quickly undid the straps, and Moses trotted whinnying into his stall, sure of what awaited him. Then the girl ran down across the field to a clump of quince bushes, whence, while not near them, she had a good view of the circus teams. She hoped the canvases might be off and possibly the lion having his dinner. Nothing so exciting met her eyes, however. The men were stretched lazily on the grass, eating cold food from unappetizing packages and pails. The dogs were sitting near, their tongues lolling, their eyes fixed on the meals whose scraps were coming to them. The ponies, half smothered in nose-bags, were snuffing and tossing their shaggy heads in determination to let no grain escape them. The horses, turned loose to browse, had wandered into the locust grove above the road, where the grass lay long and less dry than on the sunny stretch below. The thin black horse, however, looked wearily at the slight incline and turned into the road, snuffing hungrily along till he reached the corner of the orchard fence. Here a thrifty patch of meadow-prickers scratched his nose, and he raised his head and looked about in discouraged fashion.

"You poor old thing!" exclaimed Prudence. "You come right in here and take all you want." She slipped from the thicket of quince and swung the gate inward. The tall raw-boned fellow gazed in astonishment at the open space, then shambled through and dropped his head to the cool greenness.

Shortly the men rose. They harnessed the ponies again to the covered cages, and caught the horses, resting comfortably beneath the locusts. The black horse had wandered down the slope, and, by the time the cavalcade was ready to start, was hidden in the tree-shadowed ravine.

"Where's the old nag?" called one of the men roughly.

"Gone along. If we hurry, p'r'aps we'll catch up," was the jocular reply.

The first man hesitated. "Did you see him go down the road?" he questioned.

"Lucky if we lose him," advised a forth. "May die any minute, traveling like this."

"Sure! We can't treat a beast decent," stated the third man again, giving one of his team a little pat as he stood ready to clamber to his high seat. Prudence, flying across the orchard, saw the caress and made for this driver.

"Your black horse?" she cried. "He has lain down in the hollow. He's too tired to go on. Couldn't you leave him to get rested? You could get him on your way back."

The drivers stared at the excited little figure and then across the wide slope to which she pointed.

"Go after him, Tom," ordered the leader. "He'll get up all right. Anyway, we can't leave him here."

"Oh, he *is* too tired!" expostulated Prudence.

"Won't do, Sissy, to say we left him to take an afternoon nap. Fetch him up, Tom."

"Ain't wuth bringin' up," sulked Tom, by no means desirous of the race across that sunny field and the task of rousing the exhausted creature.

"What is he worth?" inquired Prudence, suddenly. "I've got five dollars. I'll buy him if that's enough."

"Take it quick!" advised the driver of the gilt coach. "Walk that horse to Deep Water, and you'll have to pay for a funeral."

The leader hesitated a moment. "All right," he agreed. "Horse is yours, Sissy."

"Oh, I'm so much obliged!" cried Prudence. The purse was empty, and the girl, who had been carefully trained to put her money in the bank, was half across the field on her way to her new possession before the men could swing themselves into their seats.

Prudence arrived at the dinner table hot and rather out of breath.

"Father," she began as she bounced into her seat, "I've borrowed two quarts of oats."

"What for?" and Mr. Kelsey paused midway in carving a slice of lamb for the newcomer.

"For my horse. I don't think I'll feed him oats much, they're so high now; but he's very weak and I thought he'd better have some today."

"I fed Moses. What are you talking about, Daughter?" and the entire family gazed at the youngest member.

"It's that black circus horse," she explained. "I let him into the orchard, and he was too tired to go on. He had lain down in the hollow, you see. So I bought him with my five dollars."

There was a gasp all round the table.

"I wish Aunt Eunice were here," said Mrs. Kelsey, after a moment of amazed silence. "She'd know now what you can do when you are left to yourself."

The twenty-one-year-old brother was looking stern disapproval, but his reproof was cut short by Mr. Kelsey's anxious inquiry: "Did the horse get up again?"

"Oh, yes!" said Prudence, very busy with her dinner. "He liked the oats and followed me to the barn, but I didn't believe he'd better have any more."

"I'm glad you bought a live horse," commented Brother Joe. "At first, I was afraid you had made a bad bargain." But satire was lost on Prudence.

"He's very friendly," she pursued. "I think he understands already that he belongs to me. Would you try him first with a saddle, Father? I'm afraid it will be some time before he can draw a wagon."

"Shouldn't wonder," agreed Joe. But Prudence was not to be teased, and the rest of the meal was somewhat silent, the family a little oppressed by the possibilities of this new acquisition, and the owner perfecting plans for the future. After dinner they all followed to the orchard, where stood the new inmate, head down, slouched on three legs, his ribs and the bones about his eyes sharply defined, his coat rough and soiled, his mane and tail tangled.

"He's a good black," encouraged Mrs. Kelsey.

"How can you tell?" inquired Joe.

"Isn't he?" agreed Prudence. "I'll wash and curry him tomorrow, but today I'm going to let him rest."

"You'll need the hose and the stepladder," advised her brother. "Are you sure you didn't buy the giraffe by mistake?"

Mr. Kelsey had been going over the animal carefully while they talked. Now he came back to the fence.

"I don't see anything the matter but overwork and underfeeding," he said. "If he isn't too tired ever to get rested, he may turn out worth all you paid for him, Prudy. But now he hasn't strength to stand up, let alone carry a saddle."

Here the horse lay down and presented a truly awful appearance, with his ungainly legs in their most ungainly position and his long neck and thin head stretched out upon the turf.

"Gracious!" was Mrs. Kelsey's comment as she gazed upon this spectacle. "I wish he could not be seen from the street till he is fed up a little."

"I wonder what tricks he did!" remarked Prudence seriously; whereat Joe cast one look at the heap of unkempt hair and bones beneath the pippin tree, and laughed uproariously.

"He'll get on now with nothing but pasturage, Daughter. How were you planning to take care of him this winter?" The farmer did not laugh like his heartless son, but there was a twinkle in his eyes as he surveyed the unpromising addition to his livestock.

"Perhaps he won't be good for much before spring," admitted Prudence, in a businesslike tone. "I thought I could earn hay enough for him, and he could just stay out in the pasture and go under the shed when it is very cold. Wild horses stay out all the time you know."

"The fresh-air cure," approved Joe. "Cheap, and nothing can hurt him."

Mr. Kelsey patted his daughter's shoulder. "That doesn't sound bad," he said. "We'll see how he gets on here for a while, anyway."

"If he's quite well next summer, I'm going to let people hire him for drives in the woods. The summer people are always trying to get the station-man's blind sorrel, and I know Roswell—I've decided to call him Roswell—will be better than that. He's got the right kind of legs to get over the ground fast."

Even Mr. and Mrs. Kelsey had to join in Joe's laughter.

"I hadn't considered Roswell as an investment," said the brother, regarding speculatively the animal that certainly looked as though it would never draw a wagon again.

"It's a good plan. I'll lend you the orchard till spring, anyway," promised her father.

So all that season the big black horse was to be seen wandering contentedly about the field. As the days grew colder, now and then he cantered round the fence line, tail up, mane blowing, quite as though he were kin to the wild horses of the pampas, whose pictures in the geography reader had caught Prudence's imagination. With the coming of winter, Joe spent more than one day making weatherproof the old shed behind the barns and opening on the orchard, and, when snow came, Roswell took possession of his quarters, and munched his hay, and stuck his head through the window opening on the farmyard to whinny a greeting to all comers, quite as though he had always been a part of the friendly Hillside Farm.

"It's 'most time to try him," announced Prudence, one spring morning. "I must be quite used to him and know all his ways before I let people hire him, and folks will want to drive out and see the boxwoods the first of June."

"You're a sure-enough business woman," encouraged the big brother, who did not care to have it known how many carrots he had stuck through Roswell's window during the course of the winter. "We'll harness him, and you can drive me to the blacksmith's. I want some bolts made, and you can get him shod."

This was a tactful way of arranging that Prudence should not take the horse out alone the first time.

"I have the money," she announced proudly. "I've done sheets and pillowcases and napkins all winter, and I guess I've got enough to take care of him till he can earn his own living."

It was no small task to fit Roswell out from the old harnesses in the barn. He watched the process with great interest and curiosity, and, if his suit looked somewhat scrappy, neither he nor his mistress was troubled. He trotted off as though the business of his life had been the drawing of little girls in runabouts.

"He certainly looks better than when he came," admitted Mrs. Kelsey, as she watched them from the steps, "but that harness needs only a bit of twine to make it the worst I've ever seen. Are you sure it's safe?"

"Safe enough. Roswell is as gentle as a kitten. Had all the spirit beaten out of him, probably. But you're right about the looks. I hate to have such a turnout belong here," and Mr. Kelsey looked ruefully after the big horse in the shabby straps.

Miss Spencer came for a few days in May. She said she came for apple blossoms and dogwood, but Prudence felt sure that Roswell was an influential factor in the unexpected visit. Roswell had ambled up and down the village streets for nearly a month, now, and everyone was used to the sight of the small girl sitting very straight in the old runabout behind the tall black horse. The family pride had dictated Prudence's birthday gift, and with Aunt Eunice from the station had come the new harness. Fortunately, the next day was Saturday, and Roswell, combed, and polished, and conscious of his honors, was brought round.

"Aunt Eunice should be pleased," remarked Mr. Kelsey, watching the horse critically as he turned up the hill towards the woods where dogwoods yet lingered. "He'll never be tough, but for five dollars, a little hay, and an unused pasture, he's not bad."

"I'm glad she didn't see him with the old traps," commented Joe, who had spent a good half hour adjusting the new leathers till they fitted to the inch.

"She certainly wouldn't have liked the other outfit. Aunt Eunice never did enjoy being conspicuous," remarked Mr. Kelsey.

"Are you sure it's quite safe?" inquired his wife, anxiously. "Prudence has never taken a long drive before, and I wouldn't have Aunt Eunice frightened for anything."

"Oh, Mother, Mother!" laughed Joe. "Prudence has driven all the month and nothing has happened."

"You're hard to suit, Nancy," and her husband smiled at her. "You were afraid of the other harness because it was too old, and of this because it's too new."

"Roswell never looked so much like a real horse before," she explained, laughing at her uneasiness. "He has seemed so ancient and subdued that nobody could be afraid of him."

"He's as tame as any cow within ten miles," scoffed the big brother. "Even Aunt Eunice can't be nervous behind him."

"We've never taken Roswell out here," Prudence explained as they turned into a narrow wood road. "He's just the horse for wood driving," she suggested as he paused to nip a branch of tender young oak leaves that hung low over the road.

"He has all the signs of a talent for that calling," agreed Miss Spencer. "How much do you charge? I shall use him often this vacation."

"I thought you would; he's so gentle. Joe says he's a real 'lady's horse'!" The great-aunt raised her eyebrows, but Prudence went on serenely, explaining the sort of carriage she could buy from her earnings.

They had followed the winding wood roads over brooks, and up long hills, and down into glens till at length they came into the turnpike, some two miles below their starting point. Here Roswell, who had ambled along in placid fashion, pricked up his ears.

"See what a well-shaped head he has," remarked his owner, and the guest, taking her eyes from a pink-blossomed tree in a dooryard, saw the dignified Roswell curvet lightly to the side of the road.

"Does he shy?" she demanded sharply.

"Oh, never!" Prudence reassured her. "He must have seen a toad or some little animal he didn't want to hurt. He's ever so kind," and she peered back along the wagon track.

The horse, his ears still in their becoming position, stepped gingerly along the street, now and then waving a forefoot slightly in the air. Prudence watched with great interest.

"What a pretty gait! Of course, it's rather slow, but it's very graceful."

"Does he do it often?" inquired the great-aunt, who had stretched out her hand, but, seeing Prudence's undisturbed face and her firm clasp on the reins, had remembered Joe's description of the steed, and suppressed her fears.

"Oh, no. I think he doesn't like this muddy road, and it is his way of walking on tiptoe."

This was an ingenious explanation; but at that moment Roswell minced sidewise into the mud, and then took up his promenade near the opposite walk. His neck arched, his head bowed to right and left, while his forehoofs waved slowly in unison with the movements of the glossy neck.

"I believe he has the blind staggers," said Miss Spencer, utterly puzzled and most uneasy as the wagon jolted irregularly in response to the extraordinary movements. "Certainly the creature is crazy."

They were at the brow of a hill, and there came into view on the road before them the Windham Fife and Drum Corps in all its regalia, with a trail of excited small boys in its wake. On hurried the "lady's horse," and fell into step beside the band, prancing slowly, waving his hoofs, and turning his head coquettishly from side to side. Neighbors, glancing from their windows at the sound of the bright music, called to others to see Prudence Kelsey's horse. Great-aunt Eunice, sadly jolted by the vehicle that responded to every wave of those black feet and every bend of that long neck, was about to call to the leader to stop the music, but a glance at her niece's delighted face made her straighten herself in her unsteady seat and endure the performance.

Down the street trotted Moses, and, recognizing his farmyard acquaintance, whinnied. Then he came on slowly, peering in mystified surprise at the scene. More astounded even than Moses, Joe drew up at the side of the road as the party came near. Prudence was too absorbed to notice him, but Great-aunt Eunice, as a side step of Roswell's brought their wheels perilously close, warned: "Don't frighten your Mother with this!"

"Want me to stop it?" he called, for not till they had passed did he recover from his astonishment enough to think of giving aid.

"Certainly not!" she retorted, looking back. "This is a regular 'lady's horse'!" And they waggled on, while other teams drew up by the roadside to watch, and the trail of children grew longer and longer. The fifers and drummers fifed and drummed as though they had but just begun their day. It was a mile to the post office where they were to disperse, and that full distance Roswell, with tossing head and daintily moving feet, sidled along to the rhythm of the march. Miss Spencer drew a breath of relief when the men mounted the post office porch and waved their hats to the small horsewoman, while Roswell, falling at once into his usual slow trot, went on up the road.

"Wasn't that splendid!" sighed Prudence. "I'm so glad you were along!"

"So am I, very!" returned the great-aunt fervently. "It's just as well he had the new harness on," and she reflected uncomfortably on what might have happened with weaker straps.

"Isn't it lucky!" agreed Prudence with enthusiasm. "How handsome he did look!"

"You weren't at all afraid?" suggested Miss Spencer, allowing herself to sit back comfortably once more.

"Well, you see Roswell is such a reasonable horse. I was sure he must know what he was about, even before I heard the band."

"You are better acquainted with him than I am," Aunt Eunice humbly admitted. "But I'm afraid this accomplishment will hurt business."

"Everybody saw him today," Prudence explained easily.

"They certainly did!" agreed the visitor.

"And they saw he didn't do any harm. But I don't mind its hurting business some," she added, turning shining eyes upon her relative. "Of course Roswell was a dear, and I should have bought him anyway, 'cause he had to be taken care of. But I was just the least bit disappointed that he didn't have any tricks. You'd never have guessed he knew anything about circuses. But now he's perfect!"

Nothing could have been less suggestive of the circus ring than the solemn horse that drew up at the gate to let Miss Spencer alight. She stood with her niece Nancy, watching the little girl as she drove on to the barn. "Aren't you glad she didn't put that money in the bank?" demanded the older lady. Mrs. Kelsey laughed.

"If you had seen Roswell when he came," she said, "you'd admit that his present condition is not due to any foresight on Prudence's part."

"I didn't expect foresight," returned Great-aunt Eunice. "There are qualities even more valuable. I wished to see if she had those, and I'm satisfied. She has."

◊◊◊

The East
END ROAD

George C. Lane

Bess Whitman had not missed a day of school that year, and did not intend that a little bad weather keep her from making it on this day. Besides she trusted Prince.

But after the northeaster struck in its fury, she almost turned back. But foolishly she kept going, and only Prince kept her from being swept out to sea.

But then she saw something further out—a shipwreck!

What should she do?

It is three miles from the East End to the village at Knowles Island Center, and in winter, when the northeast wind blows strong and the tides are unusually high, it is a hard road to travel. And yet, for all this, Bess Whitman had not missed a day at high school since the school year had started, four months before. She had reason to be proud of her record.

The East End is not quite separated from the rest of the island, except when the spring tides occur, and the East End Road, below the lifesaving station (they call it the coast guard now, of course), is awash in the breakers that beat in among the rocks on the north side. But it is usually not more than once or twice during the winter that the spring tides and a northeaster occur at the same time. Just beyond the narrows, to the east of the station, the island widens again into the broad, rolling acres of the Whitman farm, where, too, are located the cottages of a few of the fishermen.

It had been snowing nearly all night and was still snowing the following morning when Bess Whitman, having finished breakfast, had begun to get ready for school.

"You're not going to try it in this weather, are you, Sis?" asked Fred, her older brother. "Mr. Miner says he won't send the team out this morning. There's an extra high tide and the narrows are sure to be under water."

"Oh, I guess I can make it on Prince easily enough. And, besides," Bess concluded cheerfully, "Prince and I aren't afraid of a little weather."

"Oh, pshaw! You're just queering it for the rest of us; that's all," scolded Fred. "If you can make it on the pony, Professor Wheeler'll certainly wonder why we boys couldn't get there in the wagon. What if you do miss a day? Cut it out for once, can't you?"

"I'm not sure, Bessie, that you ought to attempt it this morning," considered Mrs. Whitman. "I'm afraid your father, if he was home, would be opposed to it. It's a very hard storm. If the town would only build the road a little higher," she sighed. "It's not safe as it is."

"The town's ready to if the government would only do its part," returned Bess. "The government can't be forced to spend a cent on road repairs along its strip between here and the station."

"Father says there are plenty of people who would like to live on this end of the island if only there was a decent road," put in Fred. "But then, I suppose, if there was one, I wouldn't have any excuse for not going to school today," he concluded, chuckling.

"It's a shame, I call it," resumed Mrs. Whitman. "When folks are sick, it's sometimes almost impossible to get a doctor to drive down."

Bess put on her warm, heavy coat and went out to the barn to saddle Prince. She asked no odds of her older brother in matters of this sort; she was as capable as any boy of her age.

"Don't be rash, now," warned Mrs. Whitman, as Bess started down the road to the gateway. "If the tide's too high, don't attempt to cross over, Bessie."

Prince scampered along through the snow as though he was enjoying it despite the cold. Bess looked back presently over her shoulder toward the house; but it was already lost to view in the thickly driving snow.

At frequent intervals the road was scarcely distinguishable from the snow-covered field each side; but Prince seemed sure of the way, and it was all so familiar to Bess, too, that she could have traveled it in the dark.

On the bluff, a mile beyond the house, where the road descended steeply to the narrows, the full force of the northeaster had swept it bare of snow. But the spray from the combers that were driving in among the rocks to windward had frozen when it struck the road, and twice Prince slipped and would have fallen but for Bess's sure hand at the rein.

She breathed a little sigh of relief when the descent was safely over. With her coat sleeve, she was obliged frequently to shelter her face as a fierce gust of the freezing, snow-filled gale struck her. At the narrows, the road, as far as she could see, was also bare of snow. The spindrift from the surf stung her face cruelly as it blew in from the big rocks to windward. In places, Bess noticed, the tide was already over the pony's feet.

Prince stopped a moment, some instinct, perhaps, telling him that it would be wiser to turn back. For a moment Bess considered the plan. She could not see across the narrows to the rising ground beyond; the snow was too thick for that. She wondered if it were foolhardy to keep on; but she wanted so much to be in school on time.

She urged Prince forward, and he went on again, reluctantly. It was a wild storm. The thunder of the surf among the outer rocks was appalling. The tide over the road became deeper. She admitted that it seemed scarcely safe, and, remembering her promise to her mother, she decided at last to turn back.

As she gazed for a moment to windward, a dim outline, barely discernible through the snow, attracted her attention. She could scarcely believe her eyes; but as she looked longer she was certain that she could define the bow and masts of a vessel out there in the storm, just beyond the breaking surf.

A thrill of fearful apprehension passed over her as she thought of her father and the *Nomad.* But no, it could not be the *Nomad,* she concluded. Mrs. Whitman had received a letter only the day before, telling of the fishing vessel's safe arrival at Portsmouth. Captain Whitman could not possibly have returned as soon as this.

With her back to the icy wind and stinging spray, Bess stopped a moment, horror-struck at the fate of the vessel and wondering whether there was still anyone left aboard. Presently there came to her above the roar of the surf the higher note of the ship's bell.

Could the lifesavers have learned of the wreck? she wondered; and doubted it. The last key-post of the shore patrol was more than a mile to the westward. The surfmen could not possibly have seen the vessel through the snow, and the flare of the Coston light or a rocket could not have been seen from the station.

All thought of school left her mind as she considered the awful predicament of the vessel and her crew. She must reach the station and tell Captain Simmons of the wreck—there was not a minute to lose! She was not her father's daughter if she did less.

"Come Prince," she coaxed. "We've got to cross the narrows, tide or not."

Bending her young shoulders to the fury of the gale, she urged the pony forward. He seemed to sense something of what was expected of him and started on. As the road wound in and out among the boulders of the beach, the water grew deeper still. It was nearly to the pony's knees. The surge of the seas as they advanced and receded—although the force of them was spent among the black rocks to windward—was disconcerting and made progress doubly hard for the pony.

Three times he stumbled on the loosened stones of the rough causeway, and Bess barely prevented a fall. Her hands were getting numb from the bitter cold, and her arms were heavy with the frozen spray on her coat sleeves. Used as she was to the sea, there was something truly terrifying in her situation.

On her right the froth-covered water swelled among the boulders with each driving sea; and on her left there were also the black rocks, although the water, in the lee of the roadway, surged in and out more quietly. The rising land on either end of the narrows was no longer visible through the storm. It was as though she were entirely surrounded by the vast stretch of black, ugly rocks and blacker, uglier water.

Prince stepped forward more slowly. Again and again Bess was obliged to urge him on as the surge of the rushing seas rose above his knees and the rough roadway beneath was lost to sight. It was dreadfully slow and dangerous going; and all the time with Bess was the thought of the men on the wrecked vessel and the need for haste.

"Come, Prince," she urged. "Can't you make it a bit faster, slowpoke?" Yet she knew the little fellow was doing his level best. She knew that the rocks of the roadway were hurting the pony's feet.

A sea of unusual size advanced, roaring, among the rocks. The swell of it rose menacingly almost to Prince's shoulder. The pony lost his footing and stumbled to his knees, his head for a moment under water. The surge of the big sea threatened to carry him over the road among the boulders and the deeper water to the leeward. Instantly Bess was out of the saddle, and in a moment she had Prince on his feet. He refused to take another step.

"It's no time to stop," scolded Bess. "Come!"

She took a step forward in her drenched boots and skirts as the water receded once more. The rein over her arm tightened. Prince would not stir. With the ends of the rein she whipped him smartly across the neck.

Surprised at this treatment, he started forward a few steps, limping painfully. With a cry of alarm Bess bent down and examined the injured leg. It was bleeding badly at the knee. She ran her hand over it and was certain that it was not broken.

"Well, we'll both walk then, old chum," she decided pluckily. "But we've just *got* to get there!" she concluded.

With the rein over her arm, she led the way. Hampered more than ever by the surge from the combers, the pony limped miserably behind.

"Poor old Prince!" she murmured, and for a moment she could not keep back the tears.

At first she had not thought of the awful cold of the water; but as she advanced along the rough, stony road, a numbness crept through her feet and legs, and it was dreadfully hard to keep going. Presently, like Prince, she stumbled and nearly fell. If she could only get clear of this numbing water!

"I might, I suppose, go faster without you," she said, patting the faithful animal's wet neck. "But I could never do that—never!"

Another giant sea advanced among the outer boulders, and as the wash of it rushed over the causeway, Bess reached involuntarily for Prince's neck for support. His short stout legs withstood the attack. It was all that saved her from being swept off the road. The sea subsided, and they started on again, poor Prince limping more than ever.

If we were only out of this awful water! thought Bess again. Her legs were almost too numb and weak to support her. But she stumbled gamely along, hoping each minute she would see the end of the narrows through the storm. All about them were the black rocks and the water, and the great, white flakes disappearing so silently into it.

Would the stony roadway never end? she wondered. Her feet were dreadfully tired and sore, and she was drenched to the shoulders by the surging seas. She was tempted to get into the saddle again, but had not the heart.

Presently, however, she could make out through the driving snow the rise of ground where the road left the narrows, and, a moment later, the key-house of the coast patrol on top of the rise. Safely over at last, they began the steep ascent. On the icy road it was a difficult climb. Once and again poor Prince went to his knees, and only Bess's alertness prevented another accident.

Realizing the need for haste, she tried desperately to increase the pace; but it was no use. Prince was not equal to going a bit faster.

"A mile and more to the station! We'll be too late, after all," reflected Bess, choking with disappointment. "If we could only see one of the surfmen now!"

But she knew that it might be two hours before one of them reached this end of the patrol again. And then an idea occurred to her. Wasn't there a telephone at the key-house? She was sure there must be one, and, yes, there was the wire!

She tried to open the little door. It was locked securely. She looked about on the strip of ground, bared of snow by the gale, and found a rock. Smashing open the door, she cranked the bell with stiffened fingers and put the receiver to her ear. The station answered, and a moment later she had delivered her message to Captain Simmons himself.

"And how under the sun did you ever get to the east key-house in this storm?" asked Captain Simmons, hurriedly.

"Came over with Prince; he's gone lame now, though," explained Bess.

"I'll send right down for both of ye," decided the keeper, promptly, and hung up.

A half hour later, Bess was being cared for by Mrs. Simmons in the warm, comfortable living room of the keeper's quarters, and Prince was enjoying a well-earned rest in the barn.

How Captain Simmons and his lifesavers in the surfboat took off the crew of the tern schooner *Jenny Moore* in a January northeaster at the East End is now a part of the records of the Knowles Island Station.

There is a new cement road to the East End now, well up beyond the reach of the highest tides. And it was Captain Simmons's report of the part that Bess and Prince played in the rescue of the schooner's crew that resulted in the government's building its share of the road.

◆◆◆

River RANCH

Aline Havard

Life was tough on the Wyoming and Dakota plains back in 1885. But for fifteen-year-old Maggie Fenwick it was bleaker than normal that day: her father was gone, and all ranch hands were out on the range, leaving her alone, with a band of outlaw raiders coming her way.

Did she dare ride her pony, Kit, in the midst of a fierce storm, across the Missouri River, with great sections of ice threatening to break loose at any minute?

Floyd Fenwick had spent his boyhood as a cowboy, his young manhood as a ranch foreman. It was only after he was left a widower with his ten-year-old daughter, Maggie, that he managed to buy a small North Dakota ranch and become an independent landowner. It meant hard work and sacrifice ahead, but Maggie's mother had always hoped to see her husband a rancher, and Fenwick, remembering her wish and thinking of Maggie's future, never rested until he had bought a good piece of land and a herd of cattle and had settled down in his own ranch house with his little daughter.

River Ranch stood near the western bank of the Missouri River, across from the town of Bismarck and ten miles north of it. The nearest settlements on the river's western side were the village of Mandan and the army post Fort Lincoln, six and twelve miles south. At first the ranch was a small, poor place which Fenwick and his few cowboys found hard to keep going. But steady work does wonders, and by the time Maggie was fifteen,

Fenwick's herd of cattle had grown to respectable numbers, his ranch was neat and prosperous looking, and the foreman's wife, with Maggie's help, had made the ranch house tidy and comfortable.

Both Fenwick and his daughter loved the place with an ardor that came from having had to work and plan so hard to get and keep it. They were utterly content there; they never tired of talking over ranch affairs, scheming how they could buy more cows, add a room to the ranch house, fence in a new paddock, buy better ponies for the range riders. Other topics, less pleasant, sometimes had also to engage their attention. For Maggie's fifteenth birthday came in January of the year 1885—in the midst of a time when holdups and robberies at the hands of outlaw raiders were but too frequent on Wyoming and Dakota prairies, bringing anxious hours to western travelers, and sleepless nights to ranchers with horses or cattle straying on the range.

Maggie Fenwick was small for her age, blonde and blue-eyed, with a delicate look that was quite deceptive, for she was strong and sturdy. A tireless rider and skater, she could brave cold and fatigue almost as well as her father. But Mrs. Jones, the foreman's wife, never could get it through her head that Maggie was stronger than she looked and did not need to be guarded against daily effort and responsibility. Maggie laughed at her cautions but liked the affection which prompted them. Her father was indulgent and she pretty much had her own way. It was toward the end of March 1885 that her pleasant, busy life was all at once interrupted by more responsibility than she wanted.

Fenwick, well known throughout that part of North Dakota for a good citizen and hard worker, had been made deputy sheriff of Morton County. All through the winter, he and his associates had been trying to lay hands on a bold gang of outlaws who roamed the banks of the Missouri, robbing travelers, scattering herds, giving the country a bad name for miles around. At last, Fenwick received word that a group of the robbers had been glimpsed east of Bismarck. He resolved to go without delay to Fort Lincoln, convey his warning to the commanding officer, and, from there, crossing the frozen river to Bismarck, lead a posse to the sandhills among which the outlaws were reported to be encamped.

Unluckily, the day that Fenwick got the news and resolved to start for the fort, twelve miles distant, a late snowstorm, unexpected as unwelcome, descended upon the prairie in a screaming gale of wind.

Jones, the foreman, was sick in bed with a fever, and Fenwick badly wanted to go himself with his cowboys to the western range to help herd the cattle into a valley between two sandhills which offered the young calves some shelter from the freezing wind. But duty demanded that he should at once give warning of the outlaws' nearness. His own information had come from an Indian trapper in a roundabout fashion. He dared not leave the people living in the country around Bismarck, or chance travelers over the prairie, to the mercy of the robbers. Snow was falling heavily, the day already greatly darkened, when, about noon, he mounted a sure-footed pony and set out from River Ranch. After the first few miles, he could count for guidance on the gun which it was customary to fire every two minutes from the fort, in bad weather, to direct homeward the soldier bringing mail from Mandan or Bismarck. Mrs. Jones remained in her little cabin behind the ranch buildings anxiously tending her husband. The cowboys had gone out on the range to struggle with the hard task of driving cold and unwilling cattle through the storm. When Fenwick had ridden away toward the fort, Maggie was left in the ranch house alone.

This was nothing new to her, and she found plenty to do, though she could not help pausing to gaze now and then from the windows with a troubled glance at thought of her father's errand. Perhaps the troops would not attempt to seek out so sly and wary an enemy on a day like this. Her thoughts veered to the cowboys, who must be having a hard, cold time of it. The wind shrieked and whistled, driving the snow in sheets against the panes. Maggie was amazed to see a solitary rider on a shrinking pony suddenly emerge from the snow curtain and gallop toward the ranch house door.

With one look at the rider, she rushed to the door and flung it open. A half-grown boy about her own age got stiffly down from the pony, brushed a little of the snow from his clothes, and ran indoors, while the shivering pony crouched in the lee of the veranda railing. "Ted! Ted Lewis! What's happened?" cried Maggie, catching and shaking her visitor's snow-covered sleeve.

The boy dropped down on a chair near the hearth, pulled his wet woolen cap from his head, wiped the snow off his cheeks and said stammeringly, "Gee, that fire feels good!" Then, moving away from the blaze as a caution against the sudden thawing of half-frozen fingers or toes, he added hurriedly, his eyes shining into Maggie's with reawakened excitement: "I stopped—I cut across—to tell you— But, say, where's your dad? Ain't he home?"

"No. Nobody's here but me. Go on."

"Well, I wish he was here—or somebody! Anyhow, it's this way." Ted gave a shiver of vivid recollection; a look of mingled fear and relief crossed his face. With some effort he spoke steadily. "It was like this, Mag. I was comin' up from Mandan—spent the night there with my cousins and started early this mornin' for our ranch, thinkin' to get there before it snowed hard. But you know how quick the storm came on. Pinto could hardly trot along—both of us half-blinded—and I reckon we were hours makin' five or six miles through the gale. When I judged we were gettin' near the river bend—ice or snow looks pretty much alike now, I got a glimpse of the steep bank, with trees along it—then up out of the storm pokes two horses' heads, with two riders behind. The men had their caps pulled low down and their mufflers wrapped close, and I'd never seen either of 'em. Say, Maggie, maybe you know that outlaws have been seen this side the river?"

"No—on the Bismarck side, Ted. Dad's gone to tell the fort—"

"It ain't on the Bismarck side they are; it's this side—or so it was rumored in Mandan before I left this morning. Anyway, you listen. These fellows rode up and shouted for me to stop. I did, of course, though not likin' their looks or manners. When they got closer, I saw for sure that I didn't know them—from even the little bit left to see of their faces, I knew they were strangers to this county. One of them says: 'Boy, where's River Ranch? Where's the deputy sheriff's place?'"

Maggie caught her breath, leaning eagerly forward. Ted went on:

"I was sort of taken aback, but I spluttered out somethin' about River Ranch bein' on a good ways. While I spoke, the idea of these men belongin' to the outlaws' gang first took hold of me, and I reckon I looked kind of scared, for one of the men said, speakin' quieter: 'What's the matter, sonny? We ain't goin' to hurt you. Which side o' the river is the sheriff's place? T'other side, ain't it? And are there lights in the ranch house at night?' I managed to say that, yes, there'd be lights here at night, most likely, before Pinto seemin' to feel pretty much the way I did, we took to our heels without answerin' the other question and galloped off through the storm with the men's shouts dyin' out behind us."

"But—Ted," Maggie faltered, cheeks flushed and hands unsteady, "because two men ask the way here and how they can find the place by dark, it doesn't mean that they are outlaws. Dad often has visitors who are strangers around here—cattle buyers, or people wanting him on sheriff's business. It was just two men—where were the rest? And Dad heard that the outlaws were all clear into the sandhills east of Bismarck."

"Maybe," muttered the boy, doubtfully. "I'd like fine to think that way, too. But these fellows looked pretty odd to me, and in Mandan, this morning, outlaws were talked about, this side the river. Anyway," Ted got up and began fastening his jacket and tying his muffler, "I cut short off to stop and tell you. Ain't nobody at all here but you? Where's all the men?"

"Mr. Jones is here, but he's sick. The rest are still out on the range. They'll be back any minute now."

"Well, I've got to start home before Pinto turns to an icicle. Don't like leavin' you, though, after bringin' that kind o' news. Want me to put Pinto under shelter and hang around awhile?"

"I should say not. You'd better get home while it's daylight. The boys'll be here before you've got far. There's twelve of them, and all good shots, so don't worry about us. But it was real kind of you to stop by. Wait a jiffy and I'll get you a drink of hot coffee."

Alone again in the ranch house, Maggie refused to let herself yield to vague fears. When the cowboys should return, in their self-confident company she could afford to doubt and wonder. But until then, while she watched Ted ride away, while she sat down again near the fire and warmed her cold fingers and got the sudden shiver from her blood, it would not do to think of outlaws this side the river, of their inquiries for River Ranch, of their enmity toward the courageous deputy sheriff of Morton County.

But what if this band of outlaws should find the ranch unprotected—should fire the buildings, stampede the horses, do whatever damage their malicious hands found possible? Maggie shuddered, her heart skipping a beat. It must not happen! She glanced up at the clock above the chimney. Half past three. The day was already declining. She got up and looked from the window out over the prairie. She could see some distance now, for the snowfall had lessened as suddenly as it had begun, though the wind still howled in fury. No sign of the cowboys. She thought of the Joneses in their cabin a quarter mile behind the ranch house. No help to be got there. Maggie sat down again, tried to read, to sew, gave up both, and sat pondering.

Suppose the cowboys could not get back before night—or that only two or three of them should return, the rest finding shelter in some herdsmen's cabin? Suppose her father should be kept on duty with the troops or at the sheriff's office? Suppose, lastly, that all Ted had said was true, and that the outlaws were in the neighborhood of the ranch, awaiting only nightfall or a lull in the storm to revenge themselves by fire and stampede upon their enemy?

It was strange that, in all these daunting thoughts, the fear of herself being driven out into the cold darkness was not first in Maggie's mind. First was the dread of the havoc that might meet her father's eyes when with daylight he should return to the ruined ranch—should see the wasted fruit of so much honest toil. The outlaws were birds of night, she knew—very unwilling to be seen or remembered. They did no violence upon citizens who might identify and betray them; their deeds were all secret, sneaking felonies. With the realization of the sort of enemies she had to oppose, some degree of coolness returned to Maggie's excited fancy, some courage to her trembling limbs. If there was no one else to plan against the intruders, why she must plan against them. If there was no force to put forward in defense of the ranch, stratagem might still do something. She repeated over and over the outlaw's words to Ted, 'Are there lights in the ranch house at night?'

Ted had answered this question, but the preceding one he had not answered. He had left the outlaws uncertain on which side of the river the ranch stood. They might still be uncertain. They might trust to the lights alone to guide them.

Lights—the idea possessed her, reminding her of something heard long ago. All at once she remembered.

Sam Barlow, one of the cowboys, had told her in her childhood an Indian tale of a girl who, knowing that the enemies' canoes were sweeping downstream toward the sick chieftain's wigwam, had run along the shore to plant torches, as guiding lights, a mile beyond the camp, where the swift current and foaming rapids made return impossible. This tale filled her brain now, stuck there, at first without definite meaning, then gradually becoming clear, transforming itself to her need. She started up and for an instant stood motionless, scarcely breathing, as her resolve shaped itself for action. Then, running into her bedroom, she drew on boots, jacket, muffler, gloves, and wool cap, picked up her riding crop, and went out the side door opening toward the paddock.

The snow had almost stopped falling, but the wind still blew hard. It cruelly cut Maggie's face now; it darted knifelike down her throat with every breath, as, running, she crossed the yard and neared the stables. There was dusk enough left for her to glimpse the foreman's cabin beyond the corral sheds toward the river. Prudence suggested that she tell Mrs. Jones of her intention; but she remembered the foreman's wife's cautions and warnings, and dreaded to be held back, pleaded with, tearfully dissuaded. Opposition would rob her of half her courage. She opened the stable doors and was greeted by a soft whicker from the corner where her pony, Kit, was fastened. First she searched for and found two big stable lanterns. Then, hurriedly saddling and bridling the pony, she tied the lanterns to his saddlebow, led him out, shut the doors, and mounted. Head bent over the pony's bent neck, she rode off eastward through the screaming gale, out of the corral gates, toward the river.

The Missouri's swift yellow stream was hidden under its winter mask of ice, but its uneven, hilly banks showed through the dusk, dotted with clumps of windswept trees. Maggie turned the pony's head northward along the bank, in the teeth of the wind, until they had covered about half a mile and she was stiff and numb with cold. Then, reining Kit in, she stared over the river in the falling darkness until she caught sight of a glimmering shadow, which was a big log shack standing on the far bank beside a clump of bare cottonwood trees. "That's it!" she said aloud, the wind snatching the words from her lips. The pony cocked one ear back at her. "Go on, Kit!" she urged, touching his flank with her crop. The pony descended the steep, snowy banks and stepped very unwillingly upon the frozen river.

The Missouri was not four hundred yards wide at this point, and Kit was used enough to crossing it in winter. At first, Maggie thought only that he disliked going out into the stormy darkness. But she was not halfway across—the north wind sweeping down to sear her cheeks and make the blood shudder in her veins—before she was aware that sagacious Kit had good reason for his reluctance. Mixed with the screaming wind, the ice kept up the strangest humming noise, broken by loud, sudden cracks throughout its surface. Maggie's heart began to throb with a new terror. It was late in March. Not two days before, she had heard her father remark that the river was holding well. But it was plain to her now that the spring breakup was at hand. The ice sighed and stirred under her feet. It might hold another day or two, or but another hour. Catching the pony's fear, she flicked Kit with the crop and, heedless of snow-covered ice and heavy wind, he broke into a jerky trot, slipped, caught himself, trotted on, never slackening speed until the eastern bank loomed ahead and he had scrambled up a snowy cut to the safe level of solid ground.

Near the riverbank, abandoned by a couple of summer herders, stood the shanty. Maggie got stiffly down, untied the lanterns with clumsy, numbed fingers, and entered the battered doorway. Kit, shivering and whinnying, pushed in after her. The little place seemed almost warm at first, half sheltered from the wind. Maggie felt inside her sheepskin jacket for matches with fingers so stiff that it was fully ten minutes before she had lighted the lanterns and raised one of them to look about her. In one corner stood a rough table. She dragged it to an angle best protected from the wind, set both lanterns upon it, then, after warming her hands an instant against the lanterns' sides, turned and led Kit into the open.

On the riverbank she looked back toward the shack. Through the hole cut for a window, through the broken door, light gleamed out into the heavy darkness. Maggie gave a sharp sigh and drew the pony down the bank. "That's all we can do, Kit. Now let's get home."

But the pony was quite determined not to set foot again on the river. He pulled shoreward as strongly as Maggie pulled on, and coaxings, orders, hard raps with the crop were of no avail.

"Oh, Kit!" Maggie cried, half sobbing, "the river will hold a little longer! We've got to get home! All right—I'm going."

She loosed Kit's rein, stumbled down the bank alone and out onto the ice. It was hard work walking over that slippery, snow-covered surface, forcing her way southwestward, in the crosscurrent of the gale. Twice she fell to her knees, and in the moment before she scrambled up again she could hear the ice beneath her crack and murmur, the swift water churning its way to freedom. The darkness was complete. She could but vaguely guess her way until, as she fought breathlessly onward, she heard the light pad and tap of hoofs behind her, and Kit's head was thrust against her sleeve. She threw her arms about his neck in relief and gratitude. "Oh, Kit, you darling, you wouldn't desert me! Hold steady, while I get on your back. You know the way home, pony—show me the way!"

No doubt about Kit's knowing the way, nor about his eagerness to get off the ice. He trotted on, slipped again and again, whinnied with fear, but did not pause until the western shore was reached, almost where Maggie had left it. Half a mile over the snow, and the ranch buildings gloomed out of the darkness.

Maggie longed now to reach Mrs. Jones's cabin—to see and speak with some human being. Moreover, she all at once realized that if the foreman's dwelling showed a light, all her efforts might be made fruitless. At the corral gate she turned to look out over the river. On its far side shone and twinkled two yellow beams from the lighted shack. It was the only lighted place to be seen in all that wide expanse of prairie darkness.

Maggie put Kit in the stable without unsaddling him and ran all the way to the foreman's cabin. From up the riverbank she fancied that there came faintly to her ears, borne on the wind, the sound of hoofbeats. Was it the cowboys, or— She tried to think the distant, half-imagined sounds came from the west, from toward the cattle range. Trembling, she reached and entered the cabin's unlocked door. In the little sitting room off the bedroom a small lamp stood on the floor to be out of range of the sick man's eyes. Maggie snatched it up as Mrs. Jones, astonished, ran from her husband's room.

"You, Maggie? Why, dear, you oughtn't to be out in this gale! Your pa and the boys back? I haven't left Ed's side all day."

Maggie blew out the lamp, clutched Mrs. Jones's friendly hand, and explained things as well as she could between chattering teeth. For a time she listened to Mrs. Jones's reassurances, tried to believe them, warmed herself in front of the stove, and half forgot her fears. But time passed, the cowboys did not come, and Maggie, remembering those distant hoofbeats, in fresh alarm threw open the kitchen window and leaned out into the windy darkness. A moment's anxious listening, then, with shaking voice, Maggie faltered, "Do you hear? Do you hear?"

"Isn't it—the cowboys?" Mrs. Jones whispered.

"No! Would they come from that way, or hang around the riverbank?" Faintly through the black darkness came the intermittent sound of hoofbeats, distant, muffled, borne on the wind. "It must be—the others," Maggie stammered. "They're near to where I crossed over!" A long, almost breathless pause of listening, then Maggie spoke again. "They're on the ice, Mrs. Jones! They're going across. They've seen the light—"

Maggie's teeth chattered. Mrs. Jones, shivering hard, drew down the sash. Together they crouched by the window, staring out at the river, northward to where that distant light gleamed from the far shore. And at last they saw it wink and vanish and reappear as riders passed around and in front of the shack. But the slow minutes dragged on, the cowboys still did not return, and as Maggie fancied the explosion of the outlaws' wrath and their renewed hunt for the ranch, her heart sank lower and lower.

Then all at once Mrs. Jones started up, clutched her companion's arm. "Maggie! Maggie!" she cried. "Do you hear? The river!"

No need to tell Maggie that. She had heard that thrilling, often-dreaded sound for many a year. With a giant crack and crash, with a roaring plunge, the Missouri's swift waters broke through the ice, tore and spurned it to fragments, and foamed down its mighty course in triumph. And Maggie, sinking her head on the windowsill, stifled a sob in her swelling throat. The outlaws were cut off from River Ranch better than by a thousand bolts and doors. No chance of their seeking out the Mandan bridge in the face of the general alarm. But was her father safe ashore?

Meanwhile, Fenwick had reached the fort by daylight to find that his own news conflicted with rumors that some of the outlaws had crossed to the river's western bank. It was hastily decided that troops should patrol the western shore, while Fenwick, crossing the river, should lead a sheriff's posse from Bismarck toward the sandhills on the eastern side. It was nightfall when Fenwick and his men rode northward up from Bismarck against the gale. About an hour after they had started, the outlaws, discovering with rage that they had been tricked into crossing the river to the lighted shanty, sought to retrace their steps, only to find the ice moaning and cracking beyond all possibility of forcing terrified horses upon it.

Darkness, fear, and anger are bad counselors in flight. Some of the outlaws fled safely back into the sandhills. But out of their band of twenty, about twelve fell into the sheriff's hands. Fenwick and his men had a long ride back to Bismarck with their prisoners, and it was near morning when Fenwick, grown more and more alarmed for his daughter and his ranch, found himself free to return home. The cowboys had got back to River Ranch about two hours after the breakup of the river. It was a great story which Mrs. Jones had to tell them, and which she and they repeated to Fenwick when wearily, but in happy relief, he rode up to the ranch house door.

Maggie could not trust herself to speak as she clung to her father. He, too, felt a shock of vivid realization which made his cheeks pale and his hands tremble. But, that first alarm past, his eyes lighted with a glow of honest pride. "Never mind, Daughter, never mind—it's over and we've got 'em!" he exclaimed, his voice thrilling with eager satisfaction. "And, oh, Maggie, it's worth all the scare and the danger to know I've got such a staunch little partner!"

◔◔◔

The Lone STALLION

Gil Close

If a wild horse trusted you, and you broke that trust, would it be as significant breaking the trust a human being had placed in you?
Merna wished she knew.

The first intimation that her brother had returned from his trip to Canyon City came to Merna Dunbar when she heard his pony, Paint, pawing at the gravel before the corral gate, waiting with growing impatience for its youthful master to finish the unsaddling.

At the time, Merna was preparing dinner in the spaciously cool kitchen of their adobe ranch house. Her blue eyes bright with hopeful expectancy, she lost no time in dropping her work and hurrying to the doorway to greet her brother.

Yet, despite her excitement, a premonition of fear gripped her. It was not like Larry to return from town like this. His usual arrival was punctuated by the thunder of galloping hooves and a series of wild, ear-splitting yells. Today his sedate approach could mean but one thing—something had gone wrong. And how well Merna knew what that something must be!

Early that morning Larry had saddled Paint and ridden toward Canyon City. With him had gone Merna's prayers for the success of his mission, upon which hinged the future of their Bar Q Ranch.

The entire forenoon had consisted of endless hours of anxious waiting. Now the waiting was over. But in Larry's attitude, as he walked toward the porch, Merna saw dejection that somehow chilled her heart.

"What did Dad Withers have to say?" she demanded, before Larry had even had time to reach the porch.

It took courage to ask that question. But during the long, drought-filled months that had made of the summer an ordeal of blasting heat, she had had to summon her courage so often that at last it had become a part of her daily life.

Larry paused on the steps and beat the dust from his chaps with his battered sombrero before answering. When he finally looked up, his gray eyes met and held his sister's anxious blue ones.

"Dad said it would cost us five hundred dollars to redrill that old well near the south water hole." His voice was calm, but he could not conceal the bitter disappointment that showed in his eyes.

Five hundred dollars! Why hadn't Dad said ten thousand? Either amount was equally impossible.

"Then that means we'll have to sell our cattle?"

Larry nodded. "Unless—"

He paused, and Merna wondered at the almost guilty expression that crossed his face.

"Unless what?" she urged him.

"Unless we're willing to capture the Lone Stallion and sell him to Pete Morin, the rodeo manager. He's offered me a thousand dollars for him just to use as a show horse."

An unexpected whiplash could not have produced more astonishment than that which showed on Merna's face. For a moment she stood speechless with surprise, her eyes glued to Larry's face. When at last she spoke, words came in an angry torrent.

"Do you mean to tell me that you'd break the trust that wild horse has placed in us?"

The sudden look of pain that dulled Larry's gray eyes made Merna sorry for her hasty words. But before she could speak again, he had dropped into a chair and had begun to reason with her.

"Listen, Sis," he said, trying to speak in a matter-of-fact voice. "We've got to think of something besides ourselves and our feelings toward the Lone Stallion in this matter. We still owe Uncle Dave for the cattle he sold us to start the Bar Q. If we have to sell our herd in its present unmarketable condition, it won't even bring enough to pay off that loan. By fall, they'll not only bring that much but a tidy sum besides.

"For some time Pete has been after me to capture the Lone Stallion for him. He knows that my horse, Paint, is the only animal in this part of the country fast enough to overtake him. Pete approached me again this morning after my talk with old Dad Withers."

"And you accepted," Merna finished bitterly.

Larry shook his head. "Not at the time. But Pete told me that it was a standing offer."

During the remainder of the afternoon, Merna worked in a daze. Somehow the whole idea seemed too cruel to even think about. Yet deep in her heart she knew that it was the only thing to do.

Two weeks more, Larry had said, would see the last water hole of which the Bar Q could boast completely dry. After that, what would they do for water? The thousand dollars that Pete had offered for the capture of the Lone Stallion would enable them to redrill an old well that Dad Withers had sunk in former days and which the old workman promised would still bring forth enough water for the entire herd.

Larry was right: there was no other way out. Bitterly, Merna realized that her brother's decision had not been of his own volition but had been forced upon him by dire necessity caused by the prolonged drought.

A vision of the Lone Stallion rose before her. She saw him again as she had on that day a week before, when she and Larry had ridden to the southern border of their ranch to repair the drift fence. It seemed as if the great white horse knew that the No Trespassing signs, which Larry had purposely posted along the southern border of the Bar Q, were to protect him from the continual string of horse hunters who harassed his trail. He had become less and less cautious in venturing down from his hideout in the wild mazes of the Lost Mountains. He now grazed his fill on the sturdy grama grass that grew so abundantly on the plains.

As time passed, he even accustomed himself to the sight of Larry and Merna on their ponies. His trust seemed to increase with each meeting. Of late, instead of dashing headlong into the hills at their approach, he would merely gallop to some prominent knoll where he could watch their progress with wild, curious eyes.

Dinner that evening was a dreary meal. Twice Merna tried to stir up some conversation, but each time Larry failed to respond. Only once did he speak. Glancing up when nearly finished, he said suddenly, "Sis, I feel like a traitor. The way he has learned to trust us—and now this!"

This time Merna did not reply. Despite her desire to assure Larry that she no longer blamed him for the decision which he was forced to make, she could not bring herself to talk about the capture of the Lone Stallion.

Early morning found them on the trail. There was no time to waste if the Lone Stallion was to be captured and delivered and a new well drilled before the critical water shortage at the ranch became worse than it already was. The sun was spraying shafts of crimson across the prairie when they rode out from the ranch buildings and headed southward toward the Lost Mountains, still only purple blotches against the morning sky. They rode in silence. Words could not distract from the pain that each knew filled the other's heart.

The rugged tips of the Lost Mountains had assumed a much clearer outline when Larry finally broke the silence. "I don't imagine he'll be down on the range this early. If not, we'll have to ride into the hills and haze him out to a place where I'll have a chance to run him down."

Myrna nodded.

The Lost Mountains were a veritable fortress in their own right. Few people ventured far into their wild extremities. Dry wash, blind canyons, and rugged gullies choked with rank growths of scrub oak and chaparral crisscrossed in a way to deter even the most valiant explorer.

True to Larry's prediction, the Lone Stallion was nowhere to be seen along the southern border of the Bar Q. Brother and sister continued onward, riding into the hills.

It was high noon before they caught the first glimpse of their quarry. At the time they were riding along the bottom of a deep gully that during wetter years formed the bed of a rushing mountain stream. Now only sunbaked sand muffled the footfalls of their horses.

Suddenly, while rounding a sharp bend, Larry reined quickly. Directly in their path, less than two hundred yards down the canyon, the Lone Stallion was ambling peacefully along in the same direction in which they were riding.

Larry withdrew quickly from sight, motioning Myrna to follow. "Everything's in our favor," he whispered quickly. "The wind is blowing from him to us; so he won't scent us. If I'm not mistaken, this canyon opens onto the Bar Q near our southern water hole. He's probably headed for the range right now!"

Silently as shadows, their hands ready to suppress any revealing neighs should their own mounts catch wind of the Lone Stallion, Larry and Merna followed, keeping just far enough behind their quarry to be out of sight and hearing.

A mile passed, two miles. Merna's excitement increased. She knew that they must be approaching very near to the southern border of the Bar Q.

"Wherever he's headed, he seems to know the way!" Larry whispered finally.

Hardly had the words left his lips when Merna, riding silently in advance, stopped suddenly and reined her pony back until it stood beside Larry's.

"He's stopped!" she whispered excitedly. "There's a large boulder blocking the canyon, with not enough room on either side to let him by!"

Larry was surprised. It was not like the Lone Stallion to blunder into such a trap as this. He sat silent for a moment, contemplating his chances. Then he outlined his quickly laid plans to Merna, shaking free the coils of his lariat as he spoke.

"You ride forward. I'll wait here behind this bend. As soon as the stallion sees you, he'll make a break past you, trying to run free. I'll rope him as he goes by."

Merna nodded dully. How she dreaded her part in this hateful task! For a moment she hesitated, feeling as one about to betray a friend. But with the same resolute courage that had carried her bravely through the trying months of drought, she thrust the feeling aside. Their only opportunity was at hand. Now was the time to act. Without a backward glance she spoke to her pony and rode boldly around the bend.

Immediately a shrill squeal of mingled surprise and terror rang through the canyon. Something in that wild challenge of despair gripped Larry's heart as he dismounted and waited behind the bend. His hands trembled as he shook free the remaining coils of his rope and dangled it ready at his side.

The stallion was coming nearer now, had passed Myrna on his mad dash for freedom. Larry braced his feet as the magnificent snow-white beast bore down upon him. He steeled his nerves. Like Merna, he realized that the moment of crisis had now come. If he missed, the Lone Stallion, with his faith shattered in the only human beings he'd ever trusted, would be next to impossible to ever corner again.

At just the right instant he made his cast. With the blind speed of a striking snake, the loop hissed outward. Widespread, it settled directly in the path of the oncoming stallion. At the precise instant when the great horse's hoofs struck the ground in the center of the sprawling loop, Larry braced his feet and lay back. A bone-racking jerk seemed literally to tear him apart; but, setting his teeth grimly, he held on.

The Lone Stallion, caught entirely by surprise, fell heavily as his forefeet were jerked together by the closing loop. In one lithe bound Larry appeared from his shelter. A quick flick of his wrist sent more coils of rope to embrace the flailing rear feet of the fallen horse. Before the Lone Stallion was fully aware of what had happened, he lay trussed and helpless on the ground. But the fire had not gone from his heart. He struggled fiercely, squealing, biting, lunging against the ropes that bound him.

Panting, Larry straightened from his task. He glanced around for Merna. She was nowhere in sight. As if in answer to the question that sprang into his eyes, he heard her calling him from down the canyon. Something in Merna's voice made him forget the struggling stallion and hurry toward her.

She had dismounted from her saddle, and was kneeling on the ground near the base of the great boulder that had blocked the Lone Stallion's progress. Now she stood up, smiling as Larry came forward. He noticed that she was pointing downward.

Then he saw it. Struck speechless, he could only stare. Bubbling from beneath the boulder was a goodly sized stream of sparkling spring water!

Still scarcely able to believe what he saw, Larry followed its liquid course on down the canyon to where, several hundred yards beyond, the last trace of it seeped into the thirsty sand. Then his gray eyes returned to meet Merna's happy blue ones. A smile wreathed his own face. He pointed upward to where, high above on the top of a sharp knoll, a lone tree stood outlined against the sky.

"That tree is less than a quarter of a mile from our south water hole.

That means that a few hundred feet of pipe will lead this water on through the canyon to our ranch. We won't have to drill a well after all!"

Merna nodded happily. "And this water explains what the Lone Stallion was doing in a blind canyon." For several moments Merna stood contemplating the water that bubbled so merrily at her feet. Why hadn't they realized before that the Lone Stallion had to have had someplace to drink in the wild fastness of these hills?

At last she raised her eyes to Larry's. A quizzical blue light glowed from their depths. "The thousand dollars Pete gives us for the Lone Stallion will be all profit now that we don't have to drill a well," she said.

Something in her voice made Larry laugh aloud. Grasping her hand, he started again up the canyon toward where the Lone Stallion still struggled gamely against his bonds.

One lithe bound and Larry had secured the loose end of the rope. A quick flick of his wrist was enough to free the struggling horse. Together, arm in arm, they watched the great beast lunge to his feet and race away up the canyon. The reverberating echo of his receding hoofbeats was the sweetest music that had reached their ears in a long, long time!

"His trust in us was tried but I hope not broken," Merna said a bit wistfully when the last echo had died away.

◆◆◆

In the
TOILS OF FATE

Virginia Mitchell Wheat

Elizabeth, who could ride any horse in the place, leaped up on the back of a black hunter that had just arrived the day before, and dared her brother to keep up with her.

It didn't take long before she realized she was on a runaway—and had no control at all!

There was nothing she could do but try to stay on and hope she'd live through the ordeal.

Elizabeth! Elizabeth! Race you to the crossroads," called a laughing youth from the back of a beautiful bay horse that pawed the ground restlessly as his master curbed him.

"What! You on Billy and I on Bess? I think not! You take Bess and give me Billy, and I'll race you."

"Oh, no," laughed the boy, teasingly, "Billy's too heady for you. He'd pull your hands off."

"Huh," returned Elizabeth, disdainfully; she could handle a horse better than her older brother could, and scorned argument.

"Well, we can't stand here all day, wasting time with folk who are afraid to take up our challenge, can we, Billy? Come on, get along!"

"Wait a minute," cried Elizabeth, "I'll race you, but not on Bess."

Running up to her room she slipped on a riding skirt, caught up a short whip, and was out of doors and across to the stables before her perplexed brother could think what she was up to. Then, an idea striking him, he wheeled about and rode Billy to the stable door just as Elizabeth came out leading a new black hunter that had only arrived the day before. His rolling eye, trembling nostrils, and nervously restless head were far from reassuring.

"Elizabeth!" exclaimed Ted, aghast. "What are you thinking of? You cannot ride him. Father would not let you."

"Father would let me if I asked him," said the spoiled Elizabeth, with a toss of her pretty head.

"Even if you please to break your neck? Here, Elizabeth," Ted said coaxingly, "you take Billy and I'll take Bess."

"Bess! In a race? Why, it would be a race to see who would come in last. There'd be no fun in that. No, I shall ride Terry, and I'll beat you to the crossroads, Master Ted, and back again, too."

"Elizabeth, don't be foolish," pleaded Ted. "Here, you take Billy and I'll take Terry, and we'll have the race."

"Ho, ho," laughed Elizabeth, derisively, "you must be a bad loser when you would take my very horse from under me because you know he can just leave you out of sight. No, no, Teddy, you keep your pretty Billy, and when Terry and I get to the crossroads we'll wait for you; that is, if you are not *too* far behind."

With a taunting laugh she put one foot on the railed fence beside her, vaulted lightly into the saddle, and before she could give the word Terry was off like an arrow from the bow.

The swift loping stride did not disturb Elizabeth in the least. She had been used to horses all her life, and so far had never had her confidence in them betrayed. Lifting her face to the cool rushing air, she breathed it in deep exhilarating draughts for a bit, then turned halfway in her saddle to wave her hand to Teddy.

She realized then how fast she was going. Billy was coming on, urged beyond his usual speed by Ted's unsparing whip, and yet as she looked she could see the distance increasing between them. Turning round she pulled sharply to slacken her horse's pace, but the effort seemed to have the opposite effect.

Sitting well back and catching a turn of the reins around her hands, she pulled again with long steady grip, but without avail. His mouth was as hard as nails.

A short time before she had sprained her wrist and now the unusual strain began to tell on it.

"Oh, pshaw!" she muttered. "He's just obstinate. The run can't do him any harm, and I'd better let him have his own way rather than cripple my wrist again. He'll soon tire out at this rate."

She looked back again, but Billy was not in sight. She loosed the reins from her cramped fingers, when, like lightning, Terry threw his head into the air, then down to his chest, dragging the slack of the reins from her, then, with the bit between his teeth, he dashed on with increasing speed.

For a few moments Elizabeth looked grave. She was not really alarmed, but the situation was altogether a novel one. Never in all her experience had she been run away with before. Every other horse in her father's stable knew her voice and loved it; but this one was a stranger, and if he was accustomed to being handled by men only, the sound of her voice might result in exciting him further.

He continued to run straight, with barely a swerve from the course he had set himself when he left the stable yard. The crossroads had been left far behind. (She *hadn't* waited for Teddy, and Elizabeth wondered with a smile if he would wait for *her,* and how long.)

On and on and on swept the horse. Would his pace never break! Well, it was useless to borrow trouble. She could keep her saddle under almost any condition, so that, unless he should stumble or fall, there wasn't much to worry about. She had known horses after a wild run like this to come to their senses after awhile and stand trembling and subdued from reaction.

Steadily, steadily, the great muscles moved beneath her, not with wild erratic action, yet with no suggestion of abating speed; then somehow, with the sort of sixth sense that came of being so thoroughly in sympathy with her father's horses, the belief came to her that there was method in his madness.

She had heard of horses and other animals finding their way back from incredible distances to a dearly loved home. This one had come from Wayville, just in the direction they were traveling, and more than seventy-five miles from her home. He had come all the way on the train, but despite this fact the conviction grew upon Elizabeth that by the aid of that instinct that so greatly compensates for the one human power these creatures lack, *Terry was going home.*

What should she do? What *could* she do? The thought of an involuntary and unexpected visit to a strange ranch was anything but a welcome one; still, even if she could accomplish the impossible feat of alighting safely from the back of this flying horse, how much better off would she be out in the midst of a desolate plain, with no means of conveyance back to her home or any town or village.

No, the only thing to do was to stick where she was; the horse would in time carry her to some definite place from which she could return, and, unless she could get control of him again, it was the only thing to do.

Once she leaned over, patted the heaving shoulder softly and spoke a soothing word or two, but Terry threw his head back and increased his speed, so she decided not to try that again. Frequent looks backward as well as all about the horizon showed that she and Terry were the only actors in the great arena, and the loneliness and long-continued strain began to tell on her nerves. She would have given the world for the opportunity to lean her head on Terry's neck for a good cry, but it wouldn't do. No time for empty hands or tear-dimmed eyes just now. Pulling herself erect in the saddle, she put the weakness away from her. So long as Terry kept on with this long, even pace she was perfectly safe. It was only a question of patience. Her father, fortunately, was away from home, and would probably not be home before the morrow. The thought of poor Ted and his fright weakened her most, so she decided not to think of him again until it was all over.

Suddenly her eyes flashed and quick color flew to her cheeks. They had reached the top of a gentle slope and away off in the distance, but straight across their path, she could see the long blue thread of a winding river. She laughed exultingly. That would prove Terry's Waterloo in very truth.

It was still five miles or farther away. If Terry would just keep up the strain of the last fifteen miles, he would be glad enough to halt and acknowledge himself beaten by the time he reached the riverbank and realized he had half a mile or more to swim before he could take up his wild journey again.

Then she began to plan how she would manage him when they reached the river. In all probability he would give up, and then she would have no trouble; but there was, of course, the chance that he would not, and then she would have to *make* him give up. She had better stay where she was until Terry came to some decision. It wouldn't do to allow him a chance to bolt and leave her there alone. The thing for her to do was to get that bit farther back in his mouth—then everything would be easy. She would keep him pacing for a while, that he might not cool too rapidly, then she would let him rest awhile, and *then* she would ride back triumphantly—meet Teddy, half scared to death, and nonchalantly declare to him that the race to the crossroads had proved so ridiculously short that she had gone on to the river instead; and she laughed again as she thought of the look that would be on Teddy's face.

The river! Why, they had never been that far before in all their riding, except on the train; and the distance would seem more tremendous to Teddy, who had been away to school for two years, than to her, for she had been riding every day. She hoped some of the river mud would stick to Terry's feed, so Ted could see it.

They were close enough to the river now for Elizabeth to discover, first with concern, and then with satisfaction, that it looked very different from the calm, smiling river that she had liked to see when she had crossed on the trestle above. Now it was tumbling and foaming, tossing angrily the bits of debris with which it was strewn, and altogether seemed so unlike the placid stream that Elizabeth remembered, that she wondered if indeed it were the same. Oh, yes, of course it was. There was the train trestle about a mile below them. Turbulent as it now appeared, it must have been worse before, for the ground for a long way from the river showed signs of a flood.

"Well, Terry, this is a joke on you," she laughed, realizing how more impassable Terry would find this than the placid stream she had anticipated, and she could not forbear to lean over again to venture a little pat of sympathy for his beaten state.

Terry threw his head again, broke from the long stride as his feet sank into the sodden earth, and then, without an instant's hesitation, plunged into the seething waters.

With a cry of terror Elizabeth reached over and clung frantically to his floating mane, and so together they started.

The horse's muscles were like iron, in spite of the long, continuous gallop and Elizabeth feared that the cold plunge, in his heated state, might produce paralysis; but he swam strongly and confidently, evading with skill the logs and other heavy objects that coursed swiftly on the racing tide. Once Elizabeth, forgetting herself, nearly lost her hold—a little cradle, empty, and still rocking softly in the tumbling waves, swept by, and after that she noted again and again many evidences of desolated homes. Thoroughly unnerved at last she closed her eyes and, clinging closely, trusted to Terry's strength and sagacity.

Presently she realized that he swam more feebly. The strong, propelling motion grew slower and more wearied and she ventured to open her eyes for an instant.

The tide had carried them almost to the trestle where logs and debris of all sorts were piled in inextricable confusion. If Terry was caught in that dreadful chaos, there would be no possible chance for either of them. Could he hold his own and keep out of it?

Her eyes closed again, and her lips moved prayerfully. She wondered silently what Ted and her father would do without her. Ted would go back to school in time, of course, and in a way he would forget, but Father—! No, she could not think what he would do, or how he would ever get along without her. They had always been so necessary to each other, she and her father. That was why she had never gone away to school like Ted; her father could not spare her, and so he had kept her home and taught her himself. Ever since those happy days when the pretty young mother had gone, she had been sweetheart and tyrant alike to him, as he often said; but now—!

She wondered whether they could manage to get ashore after all. But it seemed hopeless and she closed her eyes in dread.

A sudden tenseness—a new firmness in the muscles beneath her— made her sit up sharply and open her eyes again. *Terry was treading bottom!*

Her despondency was gone in a flash, and her plan of action instantly decided upon. She had been on Terry's back long enough, and when he reached land again she would slide off.

It might be a bit lonely for her for a while, but sooner or later a train would be along. Then she would have plenty of company, and, in spite of her being disheveled and penniless, she was confident of a quick trip home.

Terry's feet sloughed through the water that was now just above his fetlocks, and Elizabeth slipped nimbly from his back before he could have the chance to gather himself and resume his run. But Terry had no inclination to run now; whinnying softly, he thrust his quivering muzzle against her shoulder, and stood with legs trembling, thoroughly, completely subdued.

"Yes, Terry," she said softly, patting him soothingly, "like all the boys, you're very sorry for what you've done; but what good does that do now? Over this side of the river may suit you very well, but it doesn't suit me at all, and I don't see what we're going to do about it. Well, let us walk up to the railroad and see if that will help us any; and this time, Terry, we'll *both* walk. Oh, yes," as the nose touched her shoulder again, "I know you're terribly sorry, but somehow I think you and I will have to know each other a lot better before I'll trust you again."

"You see, Terry," fondling the nose to make the words seem less harsh. "You see; when anyone fools me once, I never can get over the notion that he'll do it again if he gets the chance, and I try never to give him a chance."

There was real comfort in talking and philosophizing to this dumb beast in her loneliness, and, somehow, his entire subjection and evident dependence on her judgment and sympathy girded her up with a sense of responsibility to new courage, so that it was, after all, a very cheerful and confident Elizabeth who stepped up on the track near the point where the long steel trestle began to span the river. Off to the north, she remembered, there had been a little settlement close to the river that afforded cheap and ready transit to its every part, or slow and rare intercourse with the outside world. It had vanished, unquestionably swept entirely away by the flood.

To the west and south were broad rolling lands with only the long shining rails of steel to reclaim them from the primitive state, and to the east the great blue trestle stretched from her very feet toward where her home lay, miles beyond the horizon.

Down where its massive piers met the water, logs and beams, barrels and debris of all sorts tossed and fought for supremacy like living things. The bridge had proved at first an obstacle to many of the drifting objects. While they halted at the unyielding bar across their path, others had hurried behind them, grappled with and crowded them, until at last a barrier had formed that defied the passage of every moving thing except the tossing, foaming water that rushed over and under it with a total disregard for everything but its own mighty power.

Farther up the river great trees had torn loose from their soil and joined the motley crowd on the river. In the center of the stream one fallen monarch, shorn of its magnificent dignity, lay with its roots like great feet kicking ridiculously into the air at every surge of the waters. Its branches were laden with strange fruit, for much of the flotsam and jetsam had found lodgment among them. By steady, continued pressure some of the swaying limbs had found a grip in the restlessly moving mass, and one hoary limb by some strange maneuver had thrust itself up between the sleepers of the trestle. There, scarred by its constant fret against the rail, crushed by the tremendous pressure behind it and the unyielding steel before it, a great section of that trestle had broken off and lay parallel to the shining rail.

Elizabeth's little scarlet-coated figure, still dripping from the river, and Terry at her elbow were the only living things in this scene of desolation. An awful loneliness surged over her soul, and her throat ached with the sobs that she stifled.

She had been trained early to habits of action and courage, and she looked about her again for inspiration. With the instinct that guided Terry in his runaway, her eyes clung insistently to the east, and home; and it was as she stood and so gazed, that the sight of the great limb on the track flashed its message of danger to her tired brain. She was directly in the path of the eastbound train and—

She turned about. As she did so, a long, shrill whistle sounded. The train was so near that the engineer had seen her on the track and had blown a warning: the roar of the waters below had drowned the sound of its coming!

There was just an instant for decision.

In a flash her jacket was off (that little scarlet jacket that father had insisted upon her wearing when she rode, so that he might see her a long way off) and she was waving it frantically.

The train was coming at high speed. Could, oh, could she stop it in time? In her excitement she ran to meet it, still waving and gesticulating.

The wheels and brakes were screaming and sparking now. It was stopping—it had stopped.

The engineer had jumped down beside her and she was explaining to him what the trouble was, but somehow she felt very vague and indefinite now, and this didn't sound like her voice at all!

Then passengers came crowding out to see what was wrong, and things began to blur before her eyes.

Faithful Terry still stood beside her, and she leaned against him for support. When, suddenly, from amid the throng of passengers alighting came the sound of the dearest voice in the world—her father's. "Elizabeth!" it said. And with wide, glad eyes, and a low, happy cry, she reached out her hands and sank into her father's arms.

◊◊◊

Betsy's
HORSE SHOW
RIBBON

Lavinia R. Davis

Betsy couldn't remember anything in her young life she'd wanted more than to win that ribbon for children under twelve.

But then, suddenly, the band struck up and Bad Boy lived up to his name. . . .

"There he is, Betsy, going around the ring now!" Johnny Travers pointed out the little hackney pony across the ring. Betsy watched as the pony came near them. It was trotting hard, throwing up its knees to its chest. As it flashed past them Betsy caught the sheen of its sleek, black sides.

"That's Bad Boy," Johnny said, turning toward his sister. "You're in luck to be riding him."

Betsy wasn't so sure. She watched the pony again as it came pounding past them. Flaherty, Martin's groom, was riding it now. Flaherty was so big that he and the pony looked top-heavy, but Bad Boy didn't seem to mind. Bad Boy acted as though he had nothing on his back at all, or something so light that it could hardly be noticed. He trotted as though he were a trotting machine, knees and hooves snapping.

As he left the ring after the class, Bad Boy made a neat, compact kick at the horse behind him. "Look!" Betsy said. "Did you see that?"

Johnny grinned. "He's full of beans," he said. "But he'll be all right this afternoon. Not scared, are you?"

Betsy shook her head. She wasn't, really. Or if she was it didn't make any difference. She was going to ride Bad Boy anyway. Hadn't she wanted to ride in a horse show all her life? And now, this summer for the first time she'd been given the chance. And it was on the Martins' pony at that, and Mr. Martin was the Master of Fox Hounds in Milldale Valley. Betsy hurried along to keep up with Johnny.

Johnny was going to ride in the jumping class for youth under eighteen. Betsy watched him get Melissa ready. Melissa was Johnny's hunter. She'd been a farm horse when he'd seen her and been convinced that she could jump. He'd finally gotten the family to buy her, and he'd been right about her jumping. Melissa had a head that made you think of a camel; she had great bony knees, and her gray coat looked flea bitten. Melissa was not beautiful, but she could jump.

Betsy held her while Johnny bridled and saddled her and then swung himself into the saddle. When Johnny did anything with a horse, it looked easy and natural and right. Johnny was as good a horseman as his father, and that was saying a good deal.

Betsy watched him go over the jumps with her heart in her mouth. She wasn't afraid that he'd fall but just that Melissa might be careless and clip the top of one of the big fences with her big feet. But Melissa outdid herself and Johnny went twice around the course without touching a jump.

About a half hour later Johnny came out of the ring with his big silver cup in his right hand. Johnny had won the youth's jumping class without anyone even being close to him!

"You win a ribbon this afternoon," Johnny said as he slid off Melissa, "and we will have something to tell Father when he gets home tomorrow."

For the first time Betsy thought of her parents. Mother was in Europe with Grandma, but Father was off on a business trip that would be over tomorrow. He would want to know every detail of how she had ridden Bad Boy.

For the rest of the morning Betsy couldn't get Bad Boy out of her mind. She was to ride him in the class for children under twelve, riding only to count. The class was coming soon, and Betsy wasn't quite sure that she was ready for it.

Johnny and Betsy lunched at the showground on frankfurters. Soon after they had finished, the grandstand began to fill up. The boxes blossomed with bright dresses and hats as people came for the afternoon.

At quarter to three Flaherty came looking for Betsy. She saw him first, but she didn't say anything. "Time to get ready," he said when he saw her. "Major Chase is the judge, and he's always through his classes sharp-like."

Betsy followed Johnny and Flaherty to the stable. Bad Boy was all ready, and Flaherty folded back his cooler and pulled it down his gleaming rump. Bad Boy's backsides were so shiny that they looked as though they had been oiled.

"I'll give you a leg up," Johnny said, and the next minute Betsy swung onto the saddle, and her knees were seeking to grip on Bad Boy's unrelenting sides.

"Walk up and down slowly," Flaherty said, "and get him used to the other children. He's not used to such big classes."

Bad Boy didn't like being in a class with nearly forty children. He threatened every horse or pony that came within six feet of his tail.

"Class 58—Best Child Rider under Twelve—this way please." The "s" of the announcer's "please" sent a little shiver down Betsy's neck. The bugle blew, and Bad Boy trotted briskly into the ring. It would have been fine, but Betsy felt that he was trotting that way because he wanted to and because the bugle made him feel frisky, and not because he was doing what she directed him to do.

The horse show grounds were filled. There were people everywhere—in the boxes, in the reserved seats, and two deep around the fence that lined the ring. They held programs, purses, gloves: a hundred and one shining objects for Bad Boy to shy at.

Before she was halfway around the ring for the first time, Betsy saw the band: twelve men in red coats carrying brass instruments. She saw them going to a little platform behind the judges' stand. In another moment they would strike up, and what would Bad Boy do then?

It happened just as she and Bad Boy passed behind them! The

bandmaster lifted up his baton. One, two, three—they crashed into "Marching through Georgia."

Bad Boy nearly turned inside out! He arched in a sharp curve to the right. Betsy could feel her legs loosen. He plunged away from the band in a series of businesslike bucks.

Betsy's seat was all gone now. She held onto the reins and grabbed shamelessly to the saddle pommel. Bad Boy curved away from the band once more and ended up with one big buck. Betsy sailed off over his head!

The ground came toward her with a rush. She held the end of her reins and fell. She hit it hard, very hard. She lay still for a second while the other horses circled some distance away from her. They were still trotting carefully, evenly around the ring. She was away behind them. None of the other children had even seen her.

Betsy sat up. The reins were still in her hands. She had held to them consciously, desperately. "You've got to learn to keep your horse when you fall," Johnny had said. "If you lose him when you take a spill in the hunting field, you're through."

Betsy stood up and walked toward Bad Boy. He stood looking at her, head down, sharp ears back. He looked a little like an irritated goat.

They were well beyond the regular line of riders behind the bandstand. Johnny and the rest of the audience had not seen her fall. The judges hadn't seen her either.

Betsy knew she didn't have any choice. When you fall off, you got on again right away as long as you could still walk. Johnny had told her that over and over again and so had Father, and there wasn't anything else to do.

Betsy shortened her reins in her left hand and reached for her stirrup with her right. "Steady now, Bad Boy," she said. "Steady."

She swung herself upward, and instantly Bad Boy bounced off. She saw the surprised face of one of the ring attendants who had run toward her when she had fallen. She was on again by the time he reached the spot! She was on again and riding toward the front part of the ring, posting carefully to Bad Boy's high trot.

For the rest of the class Bad Boy outdid himself. He trotted hard, as fast as he could, his legs hitting up toward his chin. Betsy caught her breath and tried to keep up with him. She knew her hat was on crooked and that there was dirt on her back. She wriggled her head a little and felt the cardboard disc that had her number on it. She'd kept that on by luck.

They passed the band from the front and from the back, but this time Bad Boy had nothing to say about it. He'd acted up, and now he was quite content to go past them as quickly, as efficiently as possible.

"Walk, please." The horses and children stopped trotting with varying degrees of speed. Bad Boy stopped instantly before Betsy's hand touched the reins. In another minute the announcer shouted, "Canter, please," and Bad Boy was off like a small skyrocket.

"Walk, please." The class settled unevenly to a walk. "Numbers 5, 14, 16, 37, and 7 in the middle of the ring, please."

Betsy could hardly believe her ears. They were being called into the middle of the ring. And she was one of the ones called!

She heard the announcer say something, and the rest of the class, thirty or more, trooped out of the ring. She started to look at the four other children lined up near the judges' stand. She saw Hughie Martin on one of his father's hunters—but just then Bad Boy started curvetting about, and she didn't have time to look any further. She had all she could do to keep Bad Boy anywhere near where he was meant to stand.

"Numbers 5, 14, 16, and 37 out in the ring, please." Betsy understood now. They'd kept her out, but she wasn't going to get a ribbon. Anyone on Bad Boy would be sure to be noticed, but that didn't mean you were going to get a ribbon. They were trying out the other four but not Bad Boy and herself.

They put the other children through their paces and then called them back to the center of the ring. "Number 37, first, please," the announcer called. "Number 14, number 16." Betsy began to turn Bad Boy toward the gate. "Number 7." Betsy could feel little prickers of excitement go down her back. They were calling her number. She had won a fourth! A glistening white ribbon! They couldn't have seen her fall! What would Johnny say, what would Father say when, with forty-odd children in the class, she'd won a ribbon?

But Bad Boy didn't like ribbons. When the man leaned toward him with the ribbons, he edged away curvetting like a kitten. It ended with Major Chase himself tucking the ribbon into Betsy's riding-coat pocket. "You gave a nice performance," he said. "Very."

Betsy smiled at him and followed the other horses round the ring. She should have said something about the fall. Should have told him that she had fallen when she was just behind his stand. But she couldn't. Not possibly. There wasn't time, and then there was the ribbon. Betsy could feel the round silky rosette in her pocket. After all, if the judge hadn't seen her? And it was her first ribbon.

In another minute they were all out of the ring, and Johnny was holding her bridle. "Nice work," he said, and there was a grin all over his face. "Nice work."

"Well done, Miss, very well done. That was a stiff class to be in the ribbons." Flaherty swung Betsy out of the saddle.

Betsy patted Bad Boy's nose and let Flaherty take him off. She looked after them unbelieving. Had nobody seen her fall?

"Let's see your ribbon," Johnny said, and she took it out to show it to him. It was a creamy satin rosette with Milldale Valley Horse Show written on it in gold letters. "That's wonderful," Johnny said. "When Father gets home tomorrow, he'll be awfully pleased."

Betsy put the ribbon carefully back in her pocket. She wanted it more than she'd ever wanted anything in her life. If Johnny hadn't seen her fall, maybe nobody'd seen her? She glanced at the attendant who'd run to pick her up. He didn't know her number, and anyway it meant nothing to him. Betsy felt the ribbon with the tip of her finger. Major Chase would never know that she'd fallen off. He'd never have a chance to give Betsy's ribbon to Number 5. The ribbon was Betsy's for keeps.

But the rest of the afternoon wasn't quite as much fun as Betsy had thought it would be. She and Johnny walked around the horse show grounds, and they kept meeting Major Chase. He wasn't judging after the children's class, and he and the Martins, with whom he was visiting, strolled around the temporary stables. It seemed to Betsy that they ran into them regularly every ten minutes.

Johnny and Betsy went home after the very last class of the horse show. When they got there, Johnny fastened his ribbon over Melissa's stall and put his cup on his own bureau where he could see it from his bed.

Betsy put her ribbon on the table beside her bed. But when she woke up once during the night, she didn't want to look at it. It caught the light and Betsy quickly turned the light off. She'd taken it under false pretenses.

She'd taken it without telling Major Chase that she'd fallen off when he couldn't see her.

Betsy turned over in bed. All of a sudden she knew what she had to do. She had to take that ribbon back to Major Chase the very first thing in the morning. It was a good thing he was staying with the Martins, who lived only a half mile down the road. Betsy pulled up the covers and tried to go to sleep. But she couldn't; she thought first of Major Chase's face, then Johnny's, and finally Father's.

Early in the morning before anybody else in the household was up, Betsy was out and walking along the dirt road that led to the Martins' place. It was very quiet so early in the morning, and the shadows of the maple trees were long and dark.

Betsy hurried along holding on tight to her ribbon. She hoped that Major Chase would be up and nobody else. To tell her story in front of Hughie Martin and all the others would be even more terrible.

When she got there, Major Chase was walking around the rose garden all by himself.

He looked very surprised when he saw her. "Why hello," he said. "Who are you?"

Betsy's heart sank. It was going to be harder than ever to explain. He didn't remember her. He'd seen hundreds of ponies and children in his three days of judging. How should he remember?

"I'm Betsy Travers," she said. "I rode in the children's horsemanship class yesterday. I—I—that is you gave me the fourth prize." Betsy held out the ribbon. "But you shouldn't have. You see, I—well—I fell off when you weren't looking."

She pushed the ribbon into Major Chase's large hand and started off. She wanted to run, to fly, to get out of that garden and on her way home. But Major Chase caught up to her and held onto one shoulder.

"Look here," he said. "Not so fast. I don't understand. At least not all of it. Were you the child on the black hackney?"

Betsy told him the story all over again. For the first time she felt an uncomfortable lumpy feeling in her throat. The morning was very hot, she hadn't slept much, and Major Chase wasn't helping her a bit.

When she was all through, Major Chase sat down on one of the stone benches and pulled Betsy down beside him. "And you thought that disqualified you?" he said gently. "And you came all the way up here to tell me about it?"

Betsy looked at him and nodded. "But doesn't it disqualify me?"

The major looked at her and shook his head. "It's the reason why I gave you the ribbon," he said. "I watched you take your spill, and I watched you get on again. Recovery after a fall's a big part of horsemanship."

"Then it's mine," Betsy said, "for keeps?"

"It certainly is," said Major Chase. "And I never knew a rider who deserved it more."

A few minutes later Major Chase took her home in his car. Just as they got there, Father drove up to the front porch. He and Major Chase shook hands, and then the major told him the story of Betsy's early morning visit. "You've got a daughter to be proud of," the major finished. "She's a rider and a sportsman."

"I knew it right along," Father said. "But it's nice to hear it from someone else."

Betsy held onto Father with one hand and the ribbon with the other. She could say nothing—she could only beam.

◆◆◆

RUSTY TAKES A SHORT CUT

The Story of an Outlaw Horse

Paul Ellsworth Triem

She was a rodeo star, yet everyone thought she was crazy to even think of taming the great outlaw horse that had killed a man.

She'd begun to wonder if they might be right. . . .

Across a quarter acre of stump land that separated the one-room schoolhouse from a hillside pasture, fenced with cedar rails, the new teacher dragged a heavy Mexican saddle. She was a capable-looking girl, and the hand that gripped the high, curved pommel was strong and brown. She brushed a wisp of auburn hair away from her forehead as she reached the rail fence, and swung the saddle up and across.

A moment later she had followed, and with a braided riding bridle in her left hand was approaching the other occupant of the pasture. This was a big, clean-limbed cayuse, considerably above the average size for mountain horses, and of the color known as strawberry roan; that is, there were silver hairs sprinkled through the reddish ground color of his coat.

He might have been carved out of bronze this morning, as he stood with his weight well forward, his ears erect, his eyes a little too bright and too prominent—and with his nostrils distended, so that the red blood showed in their lining.

"Steady, boy!" the newcomer greeted him.

He was steady enough. By not so much as a twitch or quiver did he show that he objected to her presence, but she felt his hostility as a subtle radiation from his magnificent body. She had felt it from the moment when she first set eyes on him, in the retinue of the Siwash from whom she had bought him. It was not imagination—Hazel McKenney had grown up among horses, and knew their moods instinctively.

She stood beside the big roan and was in the act of reaching up to lay her hand on his arched neck when the sound of a bell tinkling steadily along up the valley road caught her ears. She paused and looked in the direction of the sound.

A string of packhorses, tied nose to tail, appeared through the tangle of alders that lined the trail. They swung rhythmically along, and presently two riders plodded into view at the rear of the train. Hazel recognized them as packers attached to the logging camp twenty miles away across the foothills. It was in this camp that the men of the little community worked at this time of year.

As the riders came abreast of the corral, one of them glanced indifferently toward Hazel. His eyes wandered on to the cayuse, and he spoke suddenly to his companion. Next moment the two had reined in and were staring across the high fence at the horse.

They dismounted and came shuffling toward the fence, across which they clambered. The foremost of the pair touched his dilapidated hat respectfully.

"I beg your pardon, Miss, but we was aiming to take a look-see at that there cayuse. We kind of reckoned we seen him afore."

They walked slowly around the animal, noting his brand and trifling blemishes here and there; a crooked, diagonal scar on the right shoulder, and a cut across one flank.

"Sure, it's him!" the spokesman observed wonderingly. "Say, Miss, you wasn't calculating on riding that critter, was you? Because if you was—I wouldn't do it. That there was Mexican Joe's horse—the one that kilt him. And he sure has got one bad name in these parts!"

Hazel regarded the speaker. He was a loose-jointed, unprepossessing fellow, but there was the ring of truth in his voice.

"Tell me about it," she commanded. "How did he come to do it?"

"Well, Miss, they ain't much to tell. This critter was owned first by Abel

Sheehan—him as they used to call Colonel Dick. Sheehan was a rough customer and one night he got shot out'n his saddle. The horse run wild for some considerable time, till a man named Mexican Joe caught him up and tried to ride him. Seemed like the horse felt it was a comedown to be rid by a hombre like Joe. Leastwise, he flung the Mexican off into a serviceberry bush, and when Joe got up, he swore he'd whipbreak that cayuse if it was the last thing he done. Well, it was the last. He started in with a stock whip, and he had a piece of chain for a cracker. It was man against horse—and the horse won out. They say he came at Joe with his forefeet in the air and his teeth bared—"

Hazel's eyes were blazing. She had grown up in the foothill country, and the ordeal of whipbreaking was familiar to her by tradition. She looked at the strawberry roan with a new admiration. They had not broken his spirit.

The spokesman for the two packers eyed her anxiously.

"You sure won't try to ride him now, Miss? He ain't no lady's horse!"

Hazel flushed. She disliked masculine patronization.

"I rode Bumble Bee at the rodeo last year," she observed. "I can ride any horse. But I'll give this big fellow time. He hasn't had a fair chance."

When the packers had departed in a cloud of dust after their vanished pack train, the silvery twinkle of whose bells had long ago been lost, she continued to study the horse. He seemed to have tired of his part in the discussion, and had moved slowly away. He held his nose close to the ground. The whites of his eyes showed an ominous crescent as he rolled them toward the girl.

Hazel had plenty of time before school and in the long evenings, after the meager handful of lesson papers had been looked over, to visit the corral. Her advances toward friendship with the big roan were invariably repulsed; with dignity—he never snorted or plunged; but when he moved, it was always away from the girl perched like a chipmunk on top of the high rail fence. It was as if he said, "I won't molest you, but you mustn't trifle with me. All I ask is to be left to myself."

She counted on his curiosity, which is a component in the character of all horses, to win for her in the end. Eventually he would weaken. She tried to bribe him with harvest apples and with sweet, crisp turnips. He looked impersonally at these dainties, and if she left them on top of one of the corral posts, she found them trampled into the hard-packed dirt at her next visit.

And then drought touched the little water hole in the hillside pasture. Day by day it contracted, till there was not enough left to moisten the soft muzzle of the outlaw. With a thrill in her heart, the girl went to the house for a halter. As she climbed through the corral fence, she was singing a little song of triumph: "He's thirsty—he'll have to let me lead him down to the creek!"

To the horse she said "Steady, boy!"

Then she reached up, laid her hand on his arched neck, and a moment later had slipped the halter into place. Her heart pounded at her ribs, and again she was singing her song of triumph. He had not moved. She had conquered. The roan had accepted defeat without a struggle.

"Come on!" she commanded briskly. "We'll go get a drink."

The feeling that pulsed within her, she realized, was the human lust for mastery. She, a diminutive creature, weighing one hundred and twenty odd pounds, had conquered this outlaw—it was a victory of mind over matter. Unconsciously her respect for the roan diminished. That magnificent pose of his had been just bluff.

But as she trudged along in front of him toward the creek, the lengthened shadow of the horse loomed suddenly gigantic. If she had not been a girl of the foothill country, she would have missed the significance of this change. As it was, she leaped to the side—and the thrust of his forehoofs missed her by a matter of inches. She realized, even while her wrath was kindling, that she had jerked at the halter rope—and that he had promptly resented it.

Trembling like a leaf whipped by the wind, the girl faced him. He was looking at her, head up, ears tilted slightly forward, eyes cryptic. He seemed to be saying, "It's your move next!"

"You nasty, ungrateful brute!" Hazel cried, suddenly hysterical. "I wanted to be your friend—I wish now that Mexican Joe had flayed you alive."

He continued to regard her unwaveringly, and she imagined she could perceive a sardonic demon grinning out at her through his lustrous eyes.

A wisp of the girl's russet hair had blown across her forehead, and her own eyes were brimming with tears. The roan continued to stare down at her with a vast patience. He seemed to be assuring her that he could play this waiting game forever.

Her anger was tempestuous.

And then as she cooled from the height of her indignation, she began to feel mysteriously—began to sense—the hidden spirit of the horse. Without understanding the motives of the diminutive, tormenting creatures that surrounded him, evidently he had decided that they could not be trusted. Any means that served to hold them at bay were good. He would fight to the death rather than be cowed, beaten, broken. A great wrong had been done him; he had been taught to hate and to defy men, who should have been his friends.

"All right, old fellow," the girl whispered, her voice suddenly husky. "If you want a drink, come along. I won't jerk your rope again, ever. You were right and I was wrong!"

She moved tentatively toward the creek. The roan advanced at his swinging pace, even with her but well to the side. The rope hung slack between them.

The battle had entered the second and decisive phase. For a moment she had doubted the quality of her adversary. Now she knew that only love could conquer him—if even that was possible.

Hazel spent much of her time in the corral. Sometimes she carried with her an apple or a lump of sugar from Mrs. Pringle's kitchen. Usually she pretended not to notice the horse who nibbled suspiciously at the dried grass. He expressed his contempt for all bribery by twitching from the top rail, with his flexible upper lip, all the dainties she left there for him.

A time came when evidently he was yielding to temptation. The apples she left disappeared, and Hazel imagined he watched her with somewhat covetous eyes when she sat close to him, eating a white turnip with dramatic enjoyment. One afternoon she visited the corral with a new offering—a plump yellow carrot, carefully scrubbed. The roan looked up and stood at attention. Then he advanced by minute steps, with long pauses between. He thrust out his head inquiringly.

She held out the carrot. He yielded precipitately, grasped the offering between his chisel teeth and crunched it with huge appreciation. By the end of that week he would eat what she brought him without pretense of indifference.

One evening he met her at the fence, his soft muzzle thrust out questioningly. Hazel slid between the bars and stood up close to him. He eyed her impersonally. Then he advanced a step, his soft upper lip drawn back, his white teeth showing threateningly. She held herself without flinching—she felt that this was the crisis. He was trying her, was trying himself. He was probing for fear, and if he found it—

He thrust his head out till his bared teeth were close to her arm. Thus they stood for the longest moment the girl had ever known. Then he was rubbing his nose against her shoulder, and as he stood munching the carrot she had brought him, Hazel's hand rested on his smooth, strong neck.

There came a day when the wind blew fitfully and the first rain of the season fell in pattering drops on the shake roof of the schoolhouse. A syringa bush, growing just outside the window, ducked and swayed, and its supple branches scraped the glass with a silky, rustling sound.

Throughout the afternoon Hazel had heard the sounds of Old Man Pringle's axe, feeble, intermittent, as the old woodsman—the only man left in the little community during the fall work on the river—pecked at the pine tree he was undercutting. He had been a mighty axman in his day, but Time was undercutting him.

School had been dismissed. Still Hazel worked on at her desk, busy with her monthly report for the county superintendent. The rain fell more briskly, crackling like a sandblast against the window. In a lull she caught again the *thwack, thwack* of the axe—and then a crashing roar, the air throbbed and the ground shook with the fall of the pine. The feeble might of Old Man Pringle had conquered a century of sturdy growth. Hazel looked up from her desk, vaguely sorrowful.

She was again absorbed in her work when the sound of someone running up the path recalled her to her surroundings. The door was thrust open and Mrs. Pringle entered, her face pallid, her eyes glassy.

"Help—come quick—Father is under the tree—"

Hazel was out in the cool, damp evening, running. The older woman fell behind and the girl was racing for the cabin, sprinting on the balls of her feet. She vaulted the low fence and was across the glistening, slippery ranch yard. She could catch the outline of the tangled pine boughs, and for them she headed.

He was not under the tree. He was lying back from the splintered butt, which evidently had broken off several feet above the cut and had caromed off at a treacherous angle, as falling trees have a trick of doing. His gray hair, long untouched by the shears, straggled forlornly around his face. There was a smear of blood across his forehead.

His pulse was beating slowly, seeming to pause after each contraction and to ask if there was any use in continuing the fight. Hazel straightened his twisted arms and pushed the hair back from his temple; a grazing blow, probably not serious for a younger man. He was breathing feebly. There was a chance, if they could get a doctor in time—

As Mrs. Pringle arrived, breathless and hysterical, Hazel decided.

"We must carry him into the house, and you get some warm things around him. Have plenty of water boiling. I'll ride to town—"

She paused, struck by a new difficulty. There was not a horse in the neighborhood—except the big roan. Mechanically she stopped and gathered the old man's fragile shoulders into her arms.

A crescent moon was setting as she entered the corral, dragging the saddle after her. Rusty, for this is what she called her big roan, stood close to the bars, his arched neck and splendid head silhouetted against the shimmering underbrush. He whinnied dubiously and took a step toward her, then stopped. He had seen the saddle.

Hazel crossed over to him and laid her hand on his head.

"Steady, boy!" she said from force of habit. Then she added fiercely, as if she were striving to convince a human companion. "You've *got* to be good! You and I can save him!"

Passively the roan permitted her to slip the bit between his teeth. He lowered his head while she fastened the stiff buckle. Unresisting, he allowed her to throw a saddle blanket across his back. The saddle was in place. She pulled the girth tight and cinched it. The outlaw stood motionless. He was playing chess with her, she realized. Only he knew what move he would make when it came his turn.

Together they passed through the corral gate. The crucial moment had come. The eyes of the horse glowed down at her and his smooth neck trembled under her hand. He was a wild creature, facing ignominious servitude—she caught his mood, and her soul cried out to his. Not slavery, but partnership; her mind pierced the mists of time, and she was a nomad, communing with her free and equal companion, her horse. Man's ancient companionship with the noblest of his friends spoke from the heart of the girl to the heart of the outlaw. Her hand rested on his shoulder.

And then suddenly he dropped his nose and rubbed it against her cheek. He breathed in deeply and shook himself till the stirrups rattled. One unshod foot scraped the ground. He was ready.

She never forgot that ride. Rain clouds scudded low, apparently just above the tops of the pines. Patches of blue-black sky spangled with blazing white stars peeped intermittently out upon her. Almost directly above was Vega, a blue-white diamond; in the southwest Mars hung, murkily red, like a ship's lantern. These details the girl's eyes took in mechanically. She had been telling the round-eyed mountain children about them. In the valley lay darkness, thick and wet. Through it the roan swung forward at a tremendous pace—the spirit of the horsewoman thrilled within her, even while she was thinking of the white-haired old man back in the cabin and of the doctor far down the valley and around the spur called the Backbone. If only she could shorten the distance—if there was some way across the ridge—

Sometimes she caught the dead white of water standing in shallow puddles in the trail. At other times she heard the mountain stream gurgling and splashing in the darkness at her right. The track itself was hidden from her, but she knew she could trust to the sure vision and unfaltering foot of her mount. He was a mountain horse, descended from generations selected by ruthless nature for their skill and courage on trail and pass. Moreover, he had been the companion of Colonel Dick Sheehan, famous for his daredevil riding. She gave up all thought of guiding him, and gradually her thoughts were absorbed by other details.

She had used all the first-aid measures she was familiar with, and had told Mrs. Pringle what to do in her absence. The mill doctor would probably have to operate there in that squalid little mountain cabin—that was part of what being a doctor in the foothills implied. But first she must get him, and every moment counted. Again she seemed to feel the feeble flicker of the old man's pulse under her fingers.

A wet bough slapped her face, and involuntarily she crouched forward in the saddle. Other boughs rustled past her, and the unshod hooves of the roan struck dully against loose rocks. She perceived that they had left the level road and were climbing.

Unconsciously her hand tightened on the reins. They must have left the valley trail—there was no grade of this sort in it. She had the feeling of being pressed upon by branches: stretching out her hands, she could feel them close to her on each side! The outlaw had betrayed her; she had trusted him to follow the trail and now he had left it; she could not tell how long ago, or in what direction.

He shook his head mutinously when she strove to pull him down to a walk. He arched his neck downward in fierce negation, and she had to let him have his head. A glimmer of hope came to her: she remembered that this horse knew the foothill country as few human beings could hope to know it. Perhaps—she hardly dared articulate the idea, but she remembered her own probing wish that there might be a shortcut across the ridge. Perhaps—

He was breathing hard now. Still he drove on and up with that fierce, uncompromising gallop, but plainly he was feeling the pace. Suddenly the darkness ahead thinned to a purple luminosity, and she could see the wiry edge of the ridge outlined against the clear sky.

In the same instant she realized that her saddle was slipping. The charge up that treacherous hillside had worked the girth loose.

"Steady, boy!"

She rested her hand lightly on the reins as they came out on the level, and the roan slowed down to a walk. As she slipped from his back, the saddle veered with her. She wondered vaguely what would have happened if it had given way while they were plunging through the darkness of the lower ridge.

After she had readjusted the saddle and had tightened the girth, she walked a few steps forward along the level summit of the ridge, leading the roan. They were on the summit—there could be no doubt of that. Looking back into the turbid blackness of the farther slope she wondered that even this creature of the hills had accomplished such a journey. He must have followed an ancient trail, long unused, and somewhere in the darkness before them must lie a continuation of this trail. It would bring them out on the bank of the river above the town.

She was in the saddle, and they were driving like hunted creatures in a nightmare down a slippery, rock-strewn hillside. Stubbly fir branches scraped her cheeks, and she was drenched with water which cascaded from the saturated foliage. Once the horse stumbled and she had a sickening moment of feeling herself hurled down, down—

He caught himself and was back in the old mile-eating stride. The reins were jerked from her numb fingers, and she clung to the pommel of her saddle to avoid being scraped out by one of the overhead branches. She had become a dully conscious atom, sticking to a meteor which shot through unlighted space.

The trees thinned and receded on each side. She caught the glisten of sodden ground. They were coming out upon a bench which must be close to the river.

And then above the splashing pound of hooves she caught another sound. At first she thought it was the roar of water in a narrow, rock-bound channel. The next moment she comprehended; they were following an old trail—one that must have been in use long before the new railroad bridge was built. The horse had learned this way into town—and probably when he last used it there had been a ford where the great steel bridge stood now! The roar which shook the ground and beat with a pulse in her ears was the sound of a train coming down through the cut.

Before them two burnished, white-hot lines stood out in the darkness. They shot closer. She perceived that they were the polished rails of the track, illuminated by a distant headlight. The roan tore madly across the flat, stumbled as his feet sank into the soft earth of the embankment, and then with a snort and a shake of his head was up and was pounding down between those polished rails.

Behind them the earth shook. They were enveloped in a white glare, and the girl could see a grotesquely lengthened shadow of the horse and herself galloping ahead down the right of way. Out of the vagueness emerged a spidery scaffolding—the bridge. In the chalky radiance of the headlight she could see even the shadows cast by the slanting steel beams across the ties.

Her brain, which had been whirling, cleared in that instant. She was cool, indifferent, a little amused. The affair obviously had passed out of her hands. She held her saddle easily—that much her years of riding did for her. Now she tilted forward along the neck of the racing horse and groped for the reins. She wanted them in her hands—that was pride. When she had regained them, she straightened up in her saddle and sat staring ahead.

Behind—close behind, it seemed to the girl—a clamorous whistle sounded in one long, horrible crescendo. She distinguished above the rattle and roar another sound—a grinding of steel—as the engineer threw on the air brakes.

The bridge shot toward them. Its wide arch seemed to open like the jaws of a great, steel skull. She saw a double width of planking running between the ties, and then, for one horrible instant, she was looking down sidewise into the darkness of the river canyon.

They struck the planking and the roan's forefeet skidded. He shot forward, forelegs braced. One plunge or false motion and they would have gone over. He held himself like a horse of bronze. The training of mountain trails had taught him that trick. They caromed forward, slowed down, and were off in the same fraction of time.

No need of caution: the safest game was the boldest. The echo of the roan's pounding hoofs seemed to fill the black pit of the river valley, and to come throbbing up like muffled drums.

She closed her eyes and tightened her grip on the reins. At any rate, she would be found with her grasp on them unrelaxed—as became a rider in the rodeo.

They were across the bridge. It was impossible, but the horse had done it. Now she sawed at the reins—no need of that—he swerved, shot down the embankment and out upon a planked approach; thundered over it and across the freight platform, piled high with apple boxes; bore down upon a cluster of people who stood in front of the station, waiting for the approaching night express. The girl laughed hysterically as she saw these sedate townspeople scurry out of her way like frightened chickens.

The doctor, a portly gentleman of fifty or thereabouts, came out into the morning sunshine after an all-night vigil at the bedside of Old Man Pringle.

"He's doing nicely—considerable congestion, but we won't have to operate. He wants to see you. I told him he might thank you. And by the way—that was a rather unusual horse you rode last night. Someone told me he took a shortcut across the railroad bridge, just ahead of the evening express. Want to sell him? I suppose he's—gentle?"

Hazel's eyes twinkled.

"I suppose so," she agreed. "He killed the last man who rode him, but I'm sure he didn't intend to. I think he just wanted to maim him for life."

The doctor backed hastily away.

"Heaven save us!" he cried. "What a horrible creature—how can you bear to own him?"

"I don't!" The girl shook her head firmly. "He's free—just as free as I am. He knows it—and that's why I can ride him!"

◆◆◆

APPENDIX

My Mother's Love for "Kentucky Belle"

Joseph Leininger Wheeler

I cannot think of my dearly beloved mother, Barbara Leininger Wheeler, without also thinking about her love for story and poetry—and she loved most those that combined both, a synthesis we call "story poems." Mother was an elocutionist, a stage performer who had memorized thousands of pages of stories and poems. But out of all of them (a number, such as Alfred Noyes's "The Highwayman," Bayard Taylor's "Bedouin Love Song," and Frank Desprez's "Lasca," had to do with horses), none did she love to recite—or we children to hear—more than Constance Fennimore Woolson's "Kentucky Belle."

As I read the poem today, the cold print blurs because the words—the lines—are, in memory, watered by my mother's tears; for she could not recite this poem without crying. Because of this, because reciting it drained her so, she was always limp at the end—as were we. Yet, because of those poetic-line-induced tears, or in spite of them, our constant request remained, "Mom, please recite 'Kentucky Belle.'"

During those growing-up years, I knew little about that bloodiest of all American wars, the Civil War (a war that was anything but civil).

Nevertheless, in a very strange way, the poem so dominated my childhood that it almost predestined my career in literature, history, and biography.

To write "Kentucky Belle" today would not be possible; only someone who had lived through that gut-wrenching conflict that pitted brother against brother, and ripped families apart, could do it. Constance Fenimore Woolson, niece of that great frontier novelist, James Fenimore Cooper (author of books such as *Last of the Mohicans*), was born in March of 1840; thus she was twenty-one when the Civil War began and twenty-five when it ended. She died in 1894 at the young age of fifty-four. She was a prolific author but is remembered today mainly because she penned one of the most emotive and deeply moving poems in the English language, "Kentucky Belle." Of all the great Civil War poems that have lasted until our time, none captures more completely the torment of *both* sides than this. Nor is there another that so captures a girl-woman's heartbreak at losing the most beloved horse she would ever know.

In order to better understand this poem, we must step back in time to an age where few Americans traveled far from the place where they were born; thus they knew and loved their land with an intensity that is all but lost today. That is why this poem is such a celebration of a meandering strip of blue called the Tennessee River (the principal tributary of the Ohio, the principal eastern tributary of the Mississippi). It is born in the Appalachians near Knoxville, Tennessee, and flows southwest to Chattanooga, west through the Cumberland Plateau to northern Alabama, turns north as the boundary between Alabama and Mississippi, continuing across Tennessee and Kentucky, where it merges with the Ohio at Paducah. All the land watered by this 652-mile-long river is known as "the Tennessee." Only as we are aware of this can we fully understand this poem's poignancy to the generations of Americans who have loved both this country and the river that gives the heart of it its name.

But all this is merely a preamble to the poem itself and the horse it immortalizes.

The horse in the poem is also a metaphor for the all-consuming love a girl-woman had long ago for the Tennessee and the Kentucky Bluegrass country. Even today, when the subject of Kentucky is brought up, immediately images of the horse and the Kentucky Derby come to mind. The state and the horse are so intertwined that they are inextricable.

My mother loved Kentucky Belle the horse so much that she was a living thing to her, as real and three-dimensional to her as were her three children. And the rhythm of Woolson's lines gallops like hoofbeats through the minds of everyone who experiences the poem performed out loud by a master elocutionist such as my mother.

Now, let's drop back a century and a half to the middle of the Civil War, the summer of 1863:

Kentucky Belle

Summer of 'sixty-three, sir, and Conrad was gone away—
 Gone to the county town, sir, to sell our first load of hay.
 We lived in the log house yonder, poor as ever you've seen;
 Roschen there was a baby, and I was only nineteen.

Conrad, he took the oxen, but he left Kentucky Belle;
 How much we thought of Kentuck, I couldn't begin to tell—
 Came from the Bluegrass country; my father gave her to me
 When I rode north with Conrad, away from the Tennessee.

Conrad lived in Ohio—a German he is, you know—
 The house stood in broad cornfields, stretching on, row after row;
 The old folks made me welcome; they were kind as kind could be;
 But I kept longing, longing, for the hills of the Tennessee.

O, for a sight of water, the shadowed slope of a hill!
 Clouds that hang on the summit, a wind that never is still!

But the level land went stretching away to meet the
    sky—
Never a rise, from north to south, to rest the weary
    eye!

From east to west, no river to shine out under the
moon,
    Nothing to make a shadow in the yellow afternoon;
    Only the breathless sunshine, as I looked out, all
        forlorn,
    Only the "rustle, rustle," as I walked among the
        corn.

When I fell sick with pining we didn't wait any more,
    But moved away from the corn-lands out to this
        river shore—
    The Tuscarawas it's called, sir—off there's a hill,
        you see—
    And now I've grown to like it next best to the
        Tennessee.

I was at work that morning. Someone came riding
like mad
    Over the bridge and up the road—Farmer Rouf's
        little lad.
    Bareback he rode; he had no hat; he hardly stopped
        to say,
    "Morgan's men are coming, Fraü, they're galloping
        on this way.

"I'm sent to warn the neighbors. He isn't a mile
behind;
    He sweeps up all the horses—every horse that he
        can find;
    Morgan, Morgan the raider, and Morgan's terrible
        men,
    With bowie knives and pistols, are galloping up the
        glen."

The lad rode down the valley, and I stood still at the
door—
  The baby laughed and prattled, playing with spools
      on the floor;
  Kentuck was out in the pasture; Conrad, my man,
      was gone;
  Near, near Morgan's men were galloping, galloping
      on!

Sudden I picked up baby and ran to the pasture bar:
  "Kentuck!" I called; "Kentucky!" She knew me ever
      so far!
  I led her down the gully that turns off there to the
      right,
  And tied her to the bushes; her head was just out of
      sight.

As I ran back to the log house at once there came a
sound—
  The ring of hoofs, galloping hoofs, trembling over
      the ground,
  Coming into the turnpike out from the White-
      Woman Glen—
  Morgan, Morgan the raider, and Morgan's terrible
      men.

As near they drew and nearer my heart beat fast in
alarm;
  But still I stood in the doorway, with baby on my
      arm.
  They came; they passed; with spur and whip in
      haste they sped along;
  Morgan, Morgan the raider, and his band six
      hundred strong.

Weary they looked and jaded, riding through night
and through day;
  Pushing on east to the river, many long miles away,

To the border strip where Virginia runs up into the
    west,
And for the Upper Ohio before they could stop to
    rest.

On like the wind they hurried, and Morgan rode in
advance;
    Bright were his eyes like live coals, as he gave me a
        sideways glance;
    And I was just breathing freely, after my choking
        pain,
    When the last one of the troopers suddenly drew
        his rein.

Frightened I was to death, sir; I scarce dared look in
his face,
    As he asked for a drink of water and glanced
        around the place;
    I gave him a cup, and he smiled—'twas only a boy,
        you see,
    Faint and worn, with dim blue eyes; and he'd sailed
        on the Tennessee.

Only sixteen he was, sir—a fond mother's only son—
    Off and away with Morgan before his life had
        begun!
    The damp drops stood on his temples; drawn was
        the boyish mouth;
    And I thought me of the mother waiting down in
        the South!

O, pluck was he to the backbone and clear grit
through and through;
    Boasted and bragged like a trooper; but the big
        words wouldn't do;
    The boy was dying, sir, dying, as plain as plain
        could be,
    Worn out by his ride with Morgan up from the
        Tennessee.

But, when I told the laddie that I too was from the
South,
> Water came in his dim eyes and quivers around his
> mouth.
> "Do you know the Bluegrass country?" he wistful
> began to say,
> Then swayed like a willow sapling and fainted dead
> away.

I had him into the log house, and worked and brought
him to;
> I fed him and coaxed him, as I thought his
> mother'd do;
> And, when the lad got better, and the noise in his
> head was gone,
> Morgan's men were miles away, galloping,
> galloping on.

"O, I must go," he muttered; "I must be up and away!
> Morgan, Morgan is waiting for me! O, what will
> Morgan say?"
> But I heard a sound of tramping and kept him back
> from the door—
> The ringing sound of horses' hoofs that I had heard
> before.

And on, on came the soldiers—the Michigan
cavalry—
> And fast they rode, and black they looked galloping
> rapidly;
> They had followed hard on Morgan's track; they
> had followed day and night;
> But of Morgan and Morgan's raiders they had
> never caught a sight.

And rich Ohio sat startled through all those summer
days,
> For strange, wild men were galloping over her
> broad highways;

Now here, now there, now seen, now gone, now
    north, now east, now west,
Through river valleys and corn-land farms,
    sweeping away her best.

A bold ride and a long ride! But they were taken at last.
    They almost reached the river by galloping hard
      and fast;
    But the boys in blue were upon them ere ever they
      gained the ford,
    And Morgan, Morgan the raider, laid down his
      terrible sword.

Well, I kept the boy till evening—kept him against his
will—
    But he was too weak to follow, and sat there pale
      and still;
    When it was cool and dusky—you'll wonder to
      hear me tell—
    But I stole down to that gully and brought up
      Kentucky Belle.

I kissed the star on her forehead—my pretty, gentle
lass—
    But I knew that she'd be happy back in the old
      Bluegrass;
    A suit of clothes of Conrad's, with all the money I
      had,
    And Kentuck, pretty Kentuck, I gave to the worn-
      out lad.

I guided him to the southward as well as I knew how;
    The boy rode off with many thanks, and many a
      backward bow;
    And then the glow it faded, and my heart began to
      swell,
    As down the glen away she went, my lost Kentucky
      Belle!

When Conrad came in the evening the moon was
shining high;
    Baby and I were both crying—I couldn't tell him
        why—
    But a battered suit of rebel gray was hanging on the
        wall,
    And a thin old horse with drooping head stood in
        Kentucky's stall.

Well, he was kind, and never once said a hard word
to me;
    He knew I couldn't help it—'twas all for the
        Tennessee;
    But, after the war was over, just think what came to
        pass—
    A letter, sir; and the two were safe back in the old
        Bluegrass.

The lad had got across the border, riding Kentucky
Belle;
    And Kentuck she was thriving, and fat, and hearty,
        and well;
    He cared for her, and kept her, nor touched her
        with whip or spur:
    Ah! we've had many horses, but never a horse like
        her!

◆◆◆

ACKNOWLEDGMENTS

"Girls and Horses," by Joseph Leininger Wheeler. Copyright © 2012. Printed by permission.

"A Bluegrass Girl," by William H. Woods. Published in *St. Nicholas,* June 1913. Original text owned by Joe Wheeler.

"Oatsey Remembers," by L. R. Davis. Published in *St. Nicholas,* August 1936. Original text owned by Joe Wheeler.

"Emily Geiger," by Nina N. Selivanova. Published in *St. Nicholas,* April 1938. Original text owned by Joe Wheeler.

"Little Rhody" by Charles Newton Hood. Published in *St. Nicholas,* June 1899. Original text owned by Joe Wheeler.

"Rich but Not Gaudy," by Ruth Orendorff. Published in *Girls' Companion,* February 19, 1939. Text printed permission of Joe Wheeler (P.O. Box 1246, Conifer, CO 80433) and David C. Cook, Colorado Springs, CO 80918.

"A Satisfactory Investment," by Eveline W. Brainerd. Published in *St. Nicholas,* August 1915. Original text owned by Joe Wheeler.

"The East End Road," by George C. Lane. Published in *St. Nicholas,* August 1917. Original text owned by Joe Wheeler.

"River Ranch," by Aline Havard. Published in *St. Nicholas,* October 1925. Original text owned by Joe Wheeler.

"The Lone Stallion," by Gil Close. Published in *Young People's Weekly,* January 2, 1938. Text printed by permission of Joe Wheeler (P.O. Box 1246, Conifer, CO 80433) and David C. Cook, Colorado Springs, CO 80918.

"In the Toils of Fate," by Virginia Mitchell Wheat. Published in *St. Nicholas,* November 1907. Original text owned by Joe Wheeler.

"Betsy's Horse Show Ribbon," by Lavinia R. Davis. Published in *St. Nicholas,* October 1937. Original text owned by Joe Wheeler.

"Rusty Takes a Short Cut," by Paul Ellsworth Triem. Published in *The Christian Herald,* July 28, 1923. Published by permission of *The Christian Herald.*

"My Mother's Love for 'Kentucky Belle,'" by Joseph Leininger Wheeler. Copyright © 2012. Printed by permission. "Kentucky Belle," by Constance Fenimore Woolson. Published in *Poems of American History,* Burton Egbert Stevenson, Editor. Boston: Houghton Mifflin, 1922. Original text owned by Joe Wheeler.

◊◊◊